ADAPTED TO STRESS

The theft of classified documents, and the subsequent death of a British agent, reveal Communist activities in the United States of direct importance to the British Government. Sent to North America by the Seven Nine organisation, Simon Donahue discovers a major plan to boost Soviet technological prestige at the expense of the United States space programme. Realising that only he can prevent catastrophe, Donahue becomes involved in a series of violent events in the North-West Pacific . . .

COLIN D. PEEL

ADAPTED TO STRESS

Complete and Unabridged

LINFORD
Leicester

First published in Great Britain in 1973 by
Robert Hale and Company
London

First Linford Edition
published 2000
by arrangement with
Robert Hale Limited
London

British Library CIP Data

Peel, Colin D. (Colin Dudley) *1936 –*
Adapted to stress.—Large print ed.—
Linford mystery library
1. Detective and mystery stories
2. Large type books
I. Title
823.9'14 [F]

ISBN 0–7089–5786–2

Published by
F. A. Thorpe (Publishing)
Anstey, Leicestershire

Set by Words & Graphics Ltd.
Anstey, Leicestershire
Printed and bound in Great Britain by
T. J. International Ltd., Padstow, Cornwall

This book is printed on acid-free paper

1

The map and the description of the layby beside the road were imprinted on his mind. He knew that seeing the scrap of paper again would not really increase his confidence that he was in the correct location.

Now there was a noticeable increase in the light — was this daybreak, would they come now?

Tension began to mount rapidly inside him. David must have felt this way, or was fear a question of degree — felt more by some men than by others?

Almost instinctively he pressed closer to the ground watching dawn begin to turn the field and bordering trees to colour. The position he had chosen seemed less secure now — but nowhere was secure once the sun had risen over the hills in front of him.

Why didn't they come, damn them?

For five hours there had been no traffic

of any kind on the road. He told himself there would be none until the men he waited for arrived.

And then, faintly, but without the need for imagination, he could hear the car. It was approaching fast, probably a mile away.

A minute later, gravel crunched under the tyres of a green Chevrolet as it turned sharply onto the layby. To the man hidden in the grass on the sloping field it seemed very close.

The driver consulted a map. He had switched off the engine but remained seated inside. The windows were closed and slightly misted. Providing he remained in the car, it was unlikely that he would detect the presence of the man on the slope.

Almost at once the distant hum of another vehicle drifted down the highway, rapidly increasing in volume as it drew closer. The man in the layby had heard it too. He opened the car door.

With a muted roar, a large blue car swung round the gentle curve of the road, only to continue swiftly on its way until its sound became as imperceptible as when it had first attracted attention.

In the layby the man in the car stepped out and stretched impatiently. He wore a coarse chequered shirt, open at the neck.

Tensed like an animal, and gripping his simple weapon, the watcher waited for any sign of detection. He realized now that his position was impossible. Not only would he almost certainly be seen if he moved, but the daylight had ruined all of his plans. If he had brought the rifle as he had been told — perhaps, if he were brave, he could have managed. But how could he hope to face three men single handed from a position like this?

Under his breath he cursed the fact that the information from Seven Nine had been wrong. Just before daybreak the cable had said. Now, with daybreak well and truly gone, he was utterly helpless.

Gradually, the fear that had gripped him earlier began to dissipate.

Watching the man by the car, the creeping realization that this was one of the three that had killed David slowly

3

started to breed feelings of anger inside him. Here was a man alive on a new summers morning to feel the sun, to think of tomorrow and to enjoy today — whilst David was dead and cold forever.

Ten minutes had passed now and still there was no sign of the others. At the edge of the road the driver consulted his watch, plainly concerned that he might have missed his friends.

Still on his stomach in the grass the man made up his mind. The others weren't coming — something had caused them to change their plans. He was alone against the solitary figure staring in anticipation along the road.

Taking advantage of the driver's attitude, he gradually changed his position to a low crouch, keeping as much of his body as possible still hidden.

No sooner had he completed his move than the stocky man at the bottom of the slope turned to lean comfortably against the side of his car. Unaware that he was facing another man only yards away, he seemed to resign himself to a wait of a

4

few more minutes.

Time crept by.

The crouching man watched. If he had to keep still any longer he would scream. The muscles of his thighs ached abominably and the small of his back felt paralysed. Inside his head he shouted, 'Turn round' over and over again but seemingly to no avail.

He was shaking slightly now, trying to convince himself that it must be done, that it was right and that it must be so. There had been too long to think.

Suddenly it was time.

From inside him a long cold wave of utter calm swept outwards to the tips of his body, turning him from the frail weak thing of before to a man so filled with hate that physical control became automatic.

He rose slowly to one knee not sensing the relief of movement.

Like the flat head of a cobra, the sinister black blade of the arrow head cleared the seeded ends of the grass.

It paused and suddenly was gone, the deep hum of the powerful bow vanishing into the morning air.

After freedom of less than fifty yards the flat flight of the arrow was halted as rapidly as it had begun as six inches of steel tipped aluminium buried itself between the broad shoulders of the man in the chequered shirt, his clawing hand not reaching the small of his back before he crumpled. The dull thud of impact and his thin scream drifted back across the field.

One after another, birds that had become suddenly silent began to twitter again in the dry scrubby trees beside the road.

No change in the usual tranquil scene could be detected; there had of course been the trifling matter of a killing. The field and its inhabitants could not be expected to think of the event as special; death, which in many guises abounded in the field at all levels of life, was largely a commonplace occurrence — the passing of the man by the road was of no consequence.

The archer rose from the grass until he was standing erect, the matt dullness of his black bow merging with grey coloured shirt and jeans. He stared unmoving down the gentle slope of the field towards the road.

Now it was done. Nothing could be changed even if he wished it so.

There was a cloying sickness in his mouth and trembling of a different kind had seized him.

He unstrung his weapon.

From a buttoned shirt pocket he extracted a crumpled packet of cigarettes. The click of the lighter was the loudest sound the field had heard since the arrow had driven home a minute before.

The figure in the chequered shirt lay in a classic pose beside the old green Chevrolet parked in the layby. Face downwards, with a black shaft protruding from its back, the body appeared small and trivial against the backdrop of big country.

Leather moccasins picked their way carefully through the grass until they stood on the rough earth and grit mixture beside the road.

The shaft came out easily despite the

cruel tip; there was no blood. Only a faint ring of black dust from the soot he had used to dull the arrow showed round the slit in the shirt.

The bowman wiped the arrow three times across the shoulders of the body, then with loping strides set off along the hard tarmac of the highway towards Tacoma in the North.

He had exactly one mile to go. After less than half the distance the bow was slippery in his hand; there was no cover along the road and, although not yet six o'clock, the sun was beginning to feel warm. His relative conspicuousness could be partly reduced by disposing of the bow into the dry ditch beside the road — providing an approaching car could be heard early enough. This would hardly prevent him from being noticed though. Both his hands were black, the crushed leaves with which he had tried to remove the soot were in his pocket for he dare not drop them.

He was angry about the soot. It had taken him over an hour to dull the two arrows he carried with him on this assignment; there had not been time to do it properly with blackboard paint before leaving England. Last night the smoke from smouldering twigs had been used to temporarily dull the alloy tubes knowing that he would have to act at very early morning when perhaps stray rays of sun were about.

The fact that he had been forced to operate in daylight would not matter now — providing he reached the gas station without being seen.

As morning began to stream in brilliant shafts between the trees now lining the east side of the road, he began to imagine that cars could be heard in both directions. Small beads of perspiration ran down his forehead into his eyes.

The walker quickened his step and wondered if this would be the time his luck would fail.

For the next three hundred yards there was sufficient cover along the road behind which he could remain unseen by passing motorists — after that, five hundred yards of fenced grass land on both sides were followed by a slow left hand bend before the garage.

As the fields opened out along the roadside, he walked out of the trees and into the sunshine.

Forcing himself not to hurry and straining his ears for the sound of a distant engine he rounded the curve.

The pickup truck was still parked neatly outside the dirty white doors of what he supposed was the service bay; the door to the office was open. His plan was simple.

The gas station was scruffier than it had appeared in his headlights when he had arrived. It was still a better place to leave a vehicle overnight than on the open road or hidden where a curious highway patrol car might find it; he was pleased with his decision.

His buckskin moccasins made no sound as he approached the pickup. Quickly he opened the door to the cab and threw the bow with the two arrows behind the long bench seat. He slammed the door and turned; there was no need for the haste. Five seconds after the door had clanged shut a youth walked lazily out of the office door staring at the man by the pickup.

'Yore truck?' he asked.

'Ran out of gas — or just about — late last night. Left it here and hitched,' said the man. His speech was quiet with a soft mid-west accent.

The boy walked to the larger of the two pumps and removed a rusty padlock.

'Got enough to get this far?'

The man climbed into the pickup and started the big V8. He reversed to the pump where the boy stood with the nozzle ready.

'Fill it?'

The driver shook his head, 'Two bucks'll do it.' He held a note out of the window while the fuel gurgled in. As the filler cap was being replaced the bill fell accidentally from his fingers. 'Hell I'm sorry,' he withdrew a black hand into the cab.

The boy with a curt nod picked up the two dollars and returned to the office.

The engine coughed as the pickup turned sharply off the forecourt and pulled away up the highway towards the twin cities of Seattle and Tacoma.

Sixty miles away Mount Ranier rose splendidly through the blue haze on the horizon dominating and watching as morning finally broke over the State of Washington.

By the time the truck had passed the Tacoma turnoff on highway 99 thirty minutes later, the driver presented a rather different appearance. He had stopped beside a frothing stream which gurgled from rocks alongside the road; there in the mountain water he had cleaned his hands with mud and rinsed the sweat from his face. At the same place he had changed his clothes. The sombre grey shirt had been replaced by a white polo-necked sweater worn beneath a fawn lightweight sports jacket whilst in place of the jeans the archer now wore smart brown slacks; only the moccasins remained.

Two pieces of luggage lay on the seat beside him, both leather and both with the initials S.D. heavily embossed on the outside. One was a quality suitcase with nickel clasps, the other appeared to be a receptacle for fishing rods. The lower section of an expensive surf casting rod was tied to the outside of the leather tube, its unusual length preventing it from fitting inside the case.

Despite the relatively early hour, traffic had begun to filter onto the road, a steady stream of cars filled both lanes of the main highway. Soon the big green road signs began to occur more frequently, alternating with drive-in hamburger joints announcing themselves by coloured billboards. Neon signs left on since the night competed unsuccessfully with the morning sun now pouring through the window of the north bound truck.

Ten minutes later the truck swung left climbing the short hill to the Seattle Air Terminal building. Just before the main parking area the driver turned off the main thoroughfare stopping outside a white and yellow Hertz hut at the gate of a wire enclosure. He removed his luggage, completed the brief formalities with the tired all-night man then walked slowly to the curved white building.

There were less than eighteen minutes for things to go wrong.

At the passenger counter he smiled easily at the antiseptically smart receptionist.

'My name is Simon Donahue, I have a reservation on Flight 439 at seven twenty to Vancouver.'

The girl thought Mr Donahue would be about thirty-five and single, she checked his ticket, returned his smile and directed him to emigration. His apparent brief stay in the United States as indicated by the stamp in his soiled British Passport was not queried by the official behind the glass in the booth.

The departure lounge was empty except for the stewardess waiting at the far exit.

'All by myself?' Donahue enquired.

The girl took his boarding pass and shook her head, 'Six regulars already on board.'

He followed her out onto the apron and over to the old North Star. Inside he chose a port seat in an almost empty aircraft. He had kept both cases with

14

him — a privilege not likely to be extended on the bigger plane later on. The suitcase he put on the seat beside him letting the stewardess stow the long leather tube in the rack.

As the girl walked down the sharply sloping centre aisle to check on the seat belts of her seven passengers, the propellers began to turn. One then two, the engines spat black smoke as they burst angrily into life. The calm brown face contrasting with the white of the sweater showed no emotion. Taxiing quickly to number three runway the aircraft turned without stopping and accelerated as the pilot opened both throttles.

Simon Donahue breathed one very long quiet breath.

Ten thousand feet was an ideal altitude from which to view Puget Sound with the San Juan islands. The aircraft had climbed over Seattle and now was well on its way to the Canadian border. From the window the blue of the sea was pure Kodachrome. Anacortes, Lopez and others he could not remember — all the islands spread out below him in the

Sound. Fishing boats at the head of short white wakes dotted the blue at regular intervals; it was very beautiful.

He fought the creeping fatigue in his limbs and in his head, there was little point in sleeping until he boarded the DC8 at Vancouver. A passenger in the seat behind lit a cigarette. The click of the lighter brought the yellow field in front of Donahue as if by magic. He lit a cigarette of his own, lying back in his seat as he began to go over the events of the morning in minute detail. Attention to detail mattered a great deal in his kind of work.

Shortly after another routine inspection by the stewardess, the aircraft tipped its wings before starting on the approach to Vancouver International.

At Vancouver, Donahue ate a hurried breakfast in the cafeteria so that he would not be disturbed once he boarded the Douglas jet.

Soon the acceleration of eighty tons of aluminium and steel was pushing him back into his seat. Dimly he heard the announcement that they would be

16

cruising at 35,000 feet before thankfully slipping into a sodden sleep; Donahue had not slept for twenty-nine hours.

He did not wake at Calgary nor at Winnipeg.

At 0650 hours at terminal 3 of London airport, flight AC 532 from Vancouver disgorged its passengers. The casually dressed man with two leather cases filtered slowly through the tedium of Customs, finally passing through the glass doors out into the sunshine of another morning.

Twelve thousand miles away, a man in a chequered shirt had been found lying beside the road. He had been very stiff and very dead.

★ ★ ★

The Tacoma division of the Washington State Patrol were astonished at their own efficiency. At seven twenty-three on the morning of June the twentieth a 'phone call had been received from an obscure gas station some twenty-five miles south on route twenty-three. A passing motorist had reported what appeared to be a dead man lying on the soft shoulder beside the road.

In reality, the body beside the green Chevrolet had been noticed by several people as they sped by in their large comfortable cars. Some, consciences faintly stirring, wished to avoid becoming involved although the man lying on his face could only have been sick perhaps and in need of help. Sick or dead, others cared little either way as they went hurriedly about their business on the summer morning.

The sixth car to pass was driven by a local farmer. Blessed with a good deal more compassion than his fellow men — or was it plain curiosity — he had reversed slowly back to the layby in order to confirm his suspicions.

Within sixteen minutes of receiving the call, the police had car seven on the scene. By eight o'clock, the time and cause of death had been established, the name and address of the victim were known and the officer in charge was delighted with his progress.

Since 1961, the annual ritual slaughter

of deer and other animals during the hunting season had been slightly reduced in some States. Licences were now more difficult to obtain for people seeking sport with guns; this had saved the lives of many deer and numerous hunters. However, a special period of the season had been allocated to bowhunting. Hunters using longbows were generally more responsible than their counterparts using either high-power rifles or shotguns. To kill a deer with an arrow called for a degree of skill in both tracking and shooting that could only be acquired by those prepared to practise extensively. Thus there had been less accidents than in previous years, there had been only one or two minor incidents with arrows. It was these that allowed the cause of death to be swiftly ascertained. That the man had been killed with a hunting arrow there was no doubt. Not only would the laboratory probably be able to pin point the make of arrow, but with luck also explain the dark powder in and around the wound.

In his late forties, in apparently perfect

health, the stocky man had died almost instantaneously, unfortunately there was nothing so far that would indicate why he had been killed. A brown plastic billfold found in the back trouser pocket was not exactly bursting with useful information. It contained a current Washington driver's licence, twenty-eight dollars and a colour photograph of what seemed to be a complex arrangement of lenses and levers mounted on a metal cone. According to the licence, the dead man had been named Ronald Curtiss and had lived at eighty-seven Beachlands Avenue in Renton.

The boy had given a description of the early morning customer at the gas station giving the police the best lead they had so far.

Over the next few days the enthusiasm of the police officer assigned to the case began to wane; investigation revealed that Ronald Curtiss had been an unexceptional person in every respect. Eighty-seven Beachlands Avenue had disclosed nothing that would explain why the victim would have parked in the layby or why he should have been deliberately murdered — if indeed murder it was. The green Chevrolet had contained nothing of interest either except for a cardboard box full of polystyrene chips. No relatives mourned the departed man who, said the neighbours, had lived alone and who had done occasional odd jobs for those local people who had need of his limited skills. In short, there was nothing to allow the case to proceed.

After twelve weeks of diminishing police activity the Curtiss file was closed pending further information; no further information was expected.

The thin blue file was placed quite alone on a shelf at Headquarters. The Tacoma police had a system. The system classified murders and acts of violence by method, no one had been killed by an arrow in Washington before. They forgot the bloody opening of the Pacific Northwest many many years ago. The police had no sense of history.

2

Mournfully staring at the plastic walnut panelling of his office walls, Colonel Baxter sat uncomfortably on the edge of the swivel chair behind his desk. Over recent weeks his normally florid complexion had lost some of its colour, the change having been sufficiently gradual to pass unnoticed by most of the establishment staff.

This morning the Colonel was visibly disturbed as he waited nervously for the telephone to ring. They might call him in immediately he thought, alternatively the G.M. might choose to handle the whole thing himself.

In order that he would outwardly be confident in the event of a summons, he began to plan future security regulations that happily would now have to be made. He had been working on these ever since it happened and his report would be ready soon.

Colonel Baxter was the establishment security officer of Astra Physics. He had a staff of three women — all singularly unattractive — a salary of £2,750 a year and a company car. He considered himself very efficient.

Some of the more recent measures that the good Colonel had instituted in the interests of tighter security showed such imagination that the engineering department was filled with immense admiration.

Surrounding the plant there was now the new wire fence, the angled tops to each concrete post carrying strands of heavy barbed wire; the angled section was designed to prevent scaling of the fence. It was unfortunate to say the least that the angle faced inwards, effectively preventing any escape for the staff of Astra Physics.

Then there was the matter of the painted windows. Each window of the Drawing Office had been covered with a film of vomit green paint during one weekend. The measure was initially very successful, not because potential intruders would be henceforth prevented from photographing classified designs through the windows but because the exclusion of virtually all daylight from the office completely stopped the design work.

Of course there had been numerous more ordinary changes to the system. Now everyone wore — or were supposed to wear — large plastic badges with name and number marked on a departmental colour band. Complaints that the huge safety pin slowly perforated shirts and blouses were ignored by Colonel Baxter — 'You always get silly complaints about any new security regulation.'

The phone rang before he had finalized the new system for admitting visitors to the Plant.

He said, 'Certainly Bob,' into the receiver, picked up the file marked Y181: SECRET from his desk and walked importantly to the conference room.

Two men sat at one end of a long glass-topped table. Both were smoking, causing the Colonel to cough affectedly as he walked down the room, shoes sinking into the thick red executive pile of the carpet.

'This is Mr Baxter, our Security Officer.' The man at the head of the table flapped his hand casually in the general direction of the Colonel. The security officer smarted silently under the Mr — the General Manager had not risen above Major. He sat down facing the visitor across the table wondering if the name had been purposely forgotten in the brief introduction.

Bob Chesterman had been General Manager of Astra Physics for three years. Throughout that time, both he and the company had expanded until now the annual turnover was in excess of two million pounds whilst Mr Chesterman weighed nearly a hundred and ninety pounds. He had been responsible for the growth in the company's aerospace activity and the development contract for Y181 had been secured largely by his personal effort. Now, to some extent, his partially earned reputation for efficiency had suffered a severe blow.

'Baxter,' he said in his best board room

voice, 'There has been a turn of events in the Y181 business. We have obtained a prototype that was being built by our competitors.' The word competitors was spoken as though its use was particularly offensive.

The visitor facing the security officer straightened his shoulders and held up his hand stopping Chesterman from continuing.

'Perhaps I could explain our progress in this unfortunate matter to both of you.' The authority in the voice could not be missed.

'Neither of you will repeat any part of this conversation to anyone for reasons that are quite obvious.'

Relieved that the meeting was not apparently to be one at which he was to be heavily criticized for negligence, Colonel Baxter settled back in his chair listening with exaggerated attention to the unnamed man now speaking slowly through the cigarette smoke.

The stranger started at the very beginning giving his audience no credit for remembering logically any of the events that had preceded his visit — indeed they knew very little in reality.

The clear synopsis that followed was delivered easily and concisely with a minimum of pauses and only an occasional cough to clear the throat.

Y181 was the Ministry project code name for a £1.7M British contract under which Astra Physics had been developing a sun-seeking stable platform for missile and satellite guidance. The idea was very simple and not particularly novel. Using age-old navigational methods, a computer was combined with an optical system to use the sun as a basic reference for establishing position in space.

Deceptively simple in concept, the actual engineering was of extreme complexity calling for techniques of manufacture that unfortunately in some cases were not available in the United Kingdom. Sadly, and to the chagrin of the design engineers working on the project, optical encoders had to be bought from the States. British industry was not yet equipped to produce the thin glass discs with the fine coding etched to an accuracy of better than one ten thousandths of an inch.

After two years of electromechanical development involving some sixty qualified engineers, draughtsmen and technicians, a working prototype had been produced.

Three months ago in April, two men had been apprehended inside the perimeter wire one Saturday morning. To Colonel Baxter's everlasting credit, the appropriate authorities had been called in immediately to undertake detailed investigations. The outcome had caused one of the largest undercover industrial stirs in recent years.

No information had been given to the press and few people at Astra knew of the activity in various Government departments which had begun at once.

Twice before Chesterman had been brought up to date with the progress that the IEID had made. Apparently the two men had been unusually co-operative — although Chesterman doubted the statement having seen both of them briefly immediately after their capture.

Eventually the trail had led to California where to everyone's surprise another prototype was being quietly built to microfilmed information obtained directly from Astra Physics.

By a masterstroke of British ingenuity the American model, the drawings and the microfilm negatives had been seized one night with remarkably little effort. After transportation to the Embassy they had been simply flown to England in the big steel reinforced diplomatic bag.

If the sunseeker could be kept secret it would give the British a badly needed psychological advantage on guidance technique providing of course that the performance was equal to the design specification. Substantial overseas sales to the USA were anticipated.

The Americans were not expected to complain even if they knew who to complain to. The silence of their agents in England doubtless told them a good deal, nevertheless they were hardly in a position to make a fuss. It appeared a straightforward case of international inter-company espionage.

Baxter knew nothing of this apart from the initial apprehension of the intruders and what he had guessed; the fact that the American prototype copy with all the drawings was in safe hands was excellent news.

Chesterman on the other hand had known most of the information for some time. The Industrial Espionage Investigation Department — overseas section — had told him immediately the Embassy in Seattle had telephoned England.

The US prototype had not been sent to Astra Physics for assessment however, instead it had been retained in London.

On the second visit from the IEID Chesterman had been asked to confirm that the microfilm negatives were of Astra drawings. They were, taken obviously from the files and well illuminated while the nine hundred and eighty-three exposures were made.

Colonel Baxter had suffered badly that afternoon.

The speaker, still talking easily to the two Astra men was not from IEID. Chesterman had never seen him before. He had been told to expect him but knew nothing else.

The recent history of Y181 that he was now recounting indicated deep involvement with the whole case since its beginning. Chesterman wondered who he was; the impressive identification wallet had not been produced long enough for Chesterman to read either name or organization.

The visitor paused to light another cigarette not bothering to offer the packet to Chesterman or Baxter.

'This is the interesting bit,' he said.

'The US version is built exclusively of Russian solid state electronic components — transistors, integrated circuits, diodes, resistors, capacitors — everything!'

The partial relaxation that had been creeping comfortably over Colonel Baxter evaporated instantly. Chesterman wore a serious look more genuine than the artificial expressions carefully cultivated over the years for use at the meetings which he attended incessantly.

The man smiled at both of them.

'In view of what I have just told you, you will both realize that the matter is no longer one of simple industrial stealing. Moreover it is highly unlikely that our friends — who are very thorough — have allowed the information to be so easily recovered without good cause.

'You will appreciate that we cannot approach the American authorities without giving some indication of what we have done so far and for what reason. We do not wish the nature of Y181 to be known to them. We are left, gentlemen, with the problem of getting ourselves out of the mess we find ourselves in. I should add perhaps that we have a certain responsibility to NATO as well.'

Chesterman and Baxter remained silent.

'My name is Goddard.' The man looked at Chesterman. 'Here is my telephone number. I will of course be in touch with you later.'

He stood up brushing white cigarette ash from his trousers, the meeting was apparently closed.

'There is a great deal more that I shall not tell you. You will continue development on the project with, I trust, increased security.' There was a glance at the Security Officer. 'I do not believe you will be bothered further however.'

Mr Goddard smiled again; from the top of the long cocktail cabinet, which Chesterman had installed to add tone to the room, he retrieved his hat, opened the far door and walked out.

★ ★ ★

Driving back to London from the Astra Physics plant conveniently located in Farnborough, Goddard considered the characters of the two men that he had spent the morning with. Ordinarily he would have accepted the invitation to lunch invariably extended on visits to similar engineering establishments. On this occasion his visit had hardly been routine, also he had no wish to spend any more time than necessary with people that he found dull.

He did not believe that either man had anything to hide. They exhibited nothing but the simplest of reactions and probably lacked sufficient initiative for any involvement. Rather they were both almost childishly transparent and naive he thought.

He had not wanted to visit Farnborough at all but believed that some explanation should be offered to Chesterman if only to guard against the remote possibility of further leaks. The story that he had told this morning was largely the truth, he had however omitted the bulk of the part with which he was particularly involved.

Francis Goddard was one of three deputy heads of a unique Ministry Organization located amidst the dusty offices of Threadneedle Street in the City. He had never discovered what or who's extraordinary reasoning had caused the department to be placed in a street of Patent Attorneys chambers, he had been there more than long enough to stop wondering about it.

As the car turned onto the Hampshire A30, the diesel fumes immediately produced the familiar sulphury taste in his mouth. Heavily trafficked by trucks travelling to and from the south and West of England to the point where ordinary motoring was almost intolerable, the stink of exhausts could not escape the confines of the road and lay trapped like sewage in an open ditch.

Two more years of increasing traffic density and that will be the end he thought — still, that's what he had thought five years ago. Soon the wretched country would be subjected to the sonic bangs of Concorde too.

The thought of the aircraft already on flight trials in France and England brought his mind back to Y181.

God what a mess.

Marshall had been right about the second prototype copy in California. Guidance Systems Incorporated had indeed produced two identical Y181's to the Astra design.

By the time the first one had reached England where the unusual component content had been discovered, the small California company had seemingly vanished from San Carlos.

Only in America could you possibly build a piece of complex electronic equipment in a tiny office. By subcontracting just about all the manufacturing to the large well equipped plants around San Francisco it would have been relatively easy, if very expensive, to produce the two copies. All they would need in San Carlos would be assembly and testing facilities.

In the coded message that David Marshall had sent after the first model had been stolen from Guidance Systems, it had seemed certain that no others had been made. Marshall's second visit there had allowed him to send an open cable to Goddard in London. It read; 'GSI no longer in existence.'

Since then Marshall had found that three companies in San Francisco had supplied sub-assemblies to Guidance Systems — of more significance was the fact that there were two of each delivered and that electronic components were not fitted.

The recovered model showed slight changes to the circuits to allow the use of somewhat inferior Russian parts. Goddard had been told by smiling British experts that the response of the servos had suffered slightly as a result.

A month ago he had known for certain that a second copy prototype existed, he also knew he had to find it.

Working completely alone, Marshall had traced two members of the dissolved San Carlos company to a tiny coastal town in the state of Oregon where they appeared to be waiting for something.

After that, two further cables were received from Goddard's US representative, David Marshall. Marshall had been with the department for twelve years, the last seven in the States. He was a very good man indeed.

The first cable was comprehensive and expensive. By diligent searching, and with help from some American friends who were unnamed and presumably uninformed of the purpose of his enquiries, Marshall had made good progress.

A third member of the pseudo American organization had been located.

By the sound of it, Marshall had either been tapping the telephone lines of the Oregon beach house or had been closer in than he should have been.

The third man was located in Seattle

where he was responsible for the supply of the necessary USSR components, apparently imported secretly by Japanese logging ships. Marshall gave no indication of the reason behind this rather unusual carrier system.

The second cable was no less comprehensive, more expensive than its predecessor and much more serious.

It contained information to the effect that the second prototype was to be delivered to Seattle via the agent on June 20th. The precise location for the hand-over was included in the text — David Marshall was a thorough man. He had feared that imminent delivery to Seattle indicated that the sunseeker would soon be leaving the US. Four days before the night of the scheduled departure he intended to go into the beach house in a lone attempt to recover the equipment.

Goddard imagined what it must have been like on the hot summer night.

The shores of Oregon are vast, rock-strewn and quiet. Used only at weekends by their wealthy owners travelling on Fridays from Portland or from cities further north in Washington, small beach houses are not clustered closely together as in Europe. Instead, even in miniature towns, the houses are remote from each other either set deep in the silver coloured sand dunes and driftwood or nestled alone in the brush.

Marshall would have waited his time before going in, he would have been well prepared too.

And then . . .

On June 18th Goddard's secretary had passed him a folded slip of paper as soon as he had arrived in the office. It read; 'David Marshall dead. Highway 101. Oregon. Road accident.' It was signed by the security secretary of the British Embassy in Seattle.

Goddard swore under his breath as he drove. To a large extent it was his fault in not sending Donahue over earlier — he should have done some damn thing or other — now it was too late and Marshall was dead.

The traffic was becoming even more congested as he drew closer to the Metropolis.

Francis Goddard cleared his head of the responsibility of his job and changed into third. He slowed the car, set his teeth and entered the swirling stinking world of thrusting steel and squealing rubber.

Tomorrow he would sort out Mr Simon Donahue.

3

Two rays of sunshine had found their way through the compound screen of the cherry tree and venetian blind. Both drew narrow yellow lines across the untidy bed in the centre of the room.

One hundred yards away the drone of a hand-pushed lawn mower mixed with the barking of a dog and the distant buzz of morning traffic. Outside in the tree, birds sang to each other and hopped from branch to branch as if to see better into the window of the bedroom.

One of the rays narrowed further, creeping upwards over the bed until, squashed between the window frame and the upright of the dressing table, it was no more than a razor-slit of light.

The eyelids felt the change in illumination. Simon Donahue woke up.

He turned his head to one side on the pillow to avoid the brilliance; simultaneously the ray was extinguished as the sun moved on across the sky.

It was funny the way that your senses woke up one after another — the older you got the longer the delay. One day, he thought, the delay would be forever.

Suddenly the noise of the lawn mower stopped, leaving Donahue with nothing to listen to.

He breathed the faint sweet smell of perfume which drifted wonderfully across his face; he turned onto his side.

With her hair spread like a fan over the pillow, the girl reminded him of a picture of a mermaid that somehow or other was recalled from a children's book he had once had. She breathed easily in her sleep, the twin peaks of her tiny breasts rhythmically lifting the sheet lying softly over her body.

Donahue watched her for a long time.

She was quite alone now — nobody.

He woke up a little further and the beautiful summer morning lost a little of its fairyland charm. One day he would be able to lie in bed without searching for the reason that told him things were somehow not quite perfect. Or maybe you never got there — maybe there was always something. The trouble with waking up was that it went on just that bit too far — you should be able to stop in the hazy warm beginning before the knot in your stomach began to form and before you reached for that first mouth-fouling cigarette of the day.

He sat up very slowly, taking care not to disturb the girl.

Donahue lit his cigarette. Desperately trying not to cough and nearly dying in the process, he gave in and hacked.

Big yellow eyes with grey green flecks opened beside him. They saw the lean arms, the brown chest, the familiar crinkled face with the soft eyes and hard chin — they saw Simon Donahue.

He looked down at her.

Gradually the corners of the girl's eyes welled with tears. Donahue leant over towards her ironically reflecting on his thoughts of a moment ago about waking up.

Awkwardly propping her up against the white padded headboard of the bed, he tucked the sheets modestly around her shoulders.

'Don't Janey,' he said trying to stop it before it began.

She flung herself sideways into his arms sobbing.

Donahue held her tightly, his throat catching with part affection and part suppressed bitterness.

He swore to himself twice very quietly.

By the time his cigarette had burned to the point where he had to reach out to the ashtray on the table alongside the bed the worst had passed.

'Come on kid,' Donahue lifted her away from him.

The tears that had trickled down his chest left a cool moist rivulet behind on his skin.

She looked at him fiercely through filmy eyes red and puffy from the crying.

'Simon?'

'Give it time.'

For the second time he covered her small breasts with the sheet wondering why the hell he felt that he should.

Sitting in the bed now — oblivious

44

of the rest of the busy day outside, they talked quietly about themselves and about the future. They were even closer now, each needing the other more than either could find words to say.

He had gone straight to the flat when he had arrived back. As expected, she had been out. After the train journey from London down to Farnham he had managed to shake off the dreary soiled feeling that always follows a long flight. Donahue had left his luggage in the garage not bothering to let himself in with the key hidden under the swing door catch.

Lunch at the local public house in Castle Street had not been as enjoyable as it should have been due partially to the slow unwinding and relaxing of his body that was still not yet complete, and because he was sorely in need of Jane.

At 2.30 he had returned to the flat to find Jane home from the Farnham primary school where she was a spare time teacher. To see her again was something he had eagerly anticipated throughout the previous fifty hours — there was no sense of anti-climax.

They talked all afternoon — not about his trip, they never did. How the hell could they ever talk about that.

He wondered what she really felt about him now. She had obviously been crying a lot — probably the night before he thought. It's always worse at night.

Jane Marshall had been very close to her older brother David and Donahue had known both of them for three years; or rather had known David for that time.

David Marshall had watched the relationship develop between his sister and his colleague Simon Donahue with a sense of pleasure and complete hopelessness. Donahue quite understood; you didn't form deep associations with women if you worked for Seven Nine group — for your sake and for theirs.

To spend your spare time with the sister of another member of the department was bad form to say the very least. Donahue had frequently thought that if Goddard knew he would be very angry.

Eight months ago, after David had nearly come unstuck on the 'Flashlight' project he had come back to the UK on leave. The three of them had enjoyed a marvellous holiday in the beautiful Welsh Elan valley during a spell of quite exceptional weather. When David left to return to California Donahue had started sleeping with Jane.

Almost every weekend since then they had driven in Jane's Alfa Romeo Giulietta to some out of the way country hotel where they made long love through the winter nights wondering occasionally where it was all leading to.

Both were proudly in love, finding for the first time that the aloneness that each had carefully sought was an unnecessary and now unwanted protective shell that was difficult to shed.

He had told himself that he was a bastard, that for Jane's sake they should stop. His will was totally unable to remove the inherent selfishness telling him to derive what tenderness he could, before his life was snuffed out on some obscure overseas assignment one lonely dark night. Donahue hated himself but allowed Jane Marshall to draw out the feelings carefully suppressed over years of selfish solitude.

To Jane, Donahue was everything. Since her brother had left England twelve years ago when she was sixteen, Jane had been more or less alone except for an Aunt in Gloucester with whom she had lived for four dreary years.

An attractive lonely girl with big yellow eyes meets many men. Jane had spent eight years wondering if any man was different from any other. Then David had brought Simon down for a weekend — they worked together in town. The tall lean man had been most polite and genuinely friendly, although in a peculiar way, she had sensed that he was at pains to avoid any involvement with either her or David.

Slowly, Jane and Simon welded themselves into an emotional structure from which there was no escape even if they had wished it. Neither would move forward to the other — Donahue because of his job — Jane because she was not yet sure of the hesitant quiet man who was still part stranger.

On that foggy drizzly November night when David had left Southampton on the *Saxonia* bound for New York eight months ago, Donahue had gone back with Jane to Farnham. There the sad lonely girl having seen her only close relation leave after a brief autumn holiday had shyly asked Donahue to stay.

They had made frantic painful love on the pull down bed in the tiny lounge. The pent-up emotion of over two years was dissipated at last in a searing flare of passion.

Since then the two people had ceased to fight their feelings. Donahue, Jane knew, had something still to make him draw away on occasions — she believed it may be something to do with David — it was difficult to tell. She had stopped thinking it was a reluctance to become attached to anyone, and their relationship after that night had changed from one of affectionate wariness to one of complete and utter emotional involvement. Donahue wondered at himself and Jane wondered about Donahue and about them.

Then, four days ago, the office in London had sent a lovely soft spoken elderly gentleman down to the flat to say that David had been killed by a car in America.

Simon had come down the day after, tight-lipped and more quiet than usual, he had to leave on business immediately afterwards on the 19th, and she had been alone again until he had arrived back yesterday afternoon. Neither of them had intended making love last night but later, in the early hours of the morning, they ashamedly drowned their respective emotions in the hotness of each others bodies.

This morning they had carefully avoided talking of David or of their holiday last autumn in Wales. Both sat awkwardly in the big double bed which Jane had bought especially for Donahue last Christmas — he had been furious that she had done it.

'I've got to go to town again,' he said.

'Then what?'

'Then I'll come back of course — if I can.'

He climbed out of bed and disappeared to the bathroom.

'You're not going straight away?'

'Yep.'

'Oh Simon — what about breakfast — I haven't even got you any coffee.'

He appeared at the bedroom door and grinned at her.

'I'll have it tomorrow — breakfast I mean.'

Jane stayed in bed wondering how they could have behaved the way they did last night so little while after David had been dead. She could hear Donahue padding about the flat.

In ten minutes he was ready to leave.

'I'm off,' he said.

He sat on the edge of the bed and pulled the sheet from her breasts. Covering them gently with his hands he kissed her quickly on the lips, stood up, patted her on the head then turned swiftly and was gone.

★ ★ ★

Goddard tried to think of what he should do. The office was unbearably hot and stuffy but it became impossibly noisy if the window were opened — it made little difference anyway. Even with the curtains drawn to stop the sun shining in his eyes, the taxis could be heard shunting noisily about in the street below. The windows were grimy and the curtains stained with the smoke of a thousand cigarettes, the office of the deputy head (USA) of Seven Nine group was not at all what the occasional visitors expected.

He opened a thin dossier lying in the centre of his blotter. Several minutes passed during which Goddard chewed two indigestion pills taken from a large bottle in the top drawer of his desk. He was engrossed in his reading when the 'phone buzzed discreetly.

Without bothering to answer it he walked to his door and opened it wide.

In the outer office Simon Donahue was standing rather stupidly with a telephone receiver in his hand.

'Come on in,' said the older man.

Donahue sat in the uncomfortably deep chair on the visiting or subordinate side of the desk, already feeling at a considerable disadvantage brought about by the two feet difference in height between his head and that of his chief.

He waited politely.

'You are a stupid bastard, you are a complete and utter fool, a liability to Seven Nine and I am going to have you for this.' Francis Goddard spoke with conviction.

Donahue sat.

'I have your report — badly written — about the beach house — I find it difficult to believe that you could not have discovered more there. I also have chapter two which I find incredible. It reports on what seems to be the most irresponsible action any member of this organization has ever had the misfortune to make. You are at best a murderer.' Goddard was warming to his job.

'So was he.' Donahue spoke quietly.

'How the hell do you know?'

'David Marshall was my best friend,

I've known him for three years. Someone drove a truck over him on Highway 101 and I felt I should sort it out.'

'Sort it out,' Goddard shouted, 'that's what you were supposed to do — sort it out.'

Donahue attempted to reach at least level terms by sitting up very straight in the sloping chair.

'Look,' he said, 'I went to the beach, I did the place according to the book. No, Y181, no papers — nothing — not a damn thing. So I motored up to Tacoma where the hand-over was supposed to happen, hoping to get onto something there. The thing obviously wasn't going to be delivered — David may have had to tell them he knew about it — so I figured they'd called it off. Anyway, the Seattle guy turned up and waited — he obviously hadn't been told. I waited, then I killed him.'

'You mean so it's one each,' Goddard almost sneered.

Donahue said nothing.

'A twentieth century Robin Hood.'

There was a long pause as the two men

stared at each other. Finally Goddard slumped back in his chair.

Donahue lit a cigarette. 'Well?' he said.

'You're going to have to go back.'

Goddard opened the dossier again and stared at the pink pages.

'David Marshall was a friend of mine as well — I knew his father too, in the war,' Goddard paused. 'If you had perhaps had a chat with Curtiss we would be a little further along the line don't you think — especially with regard to finding out exactly what happened to David.

'You are going in again to find out where the hell Y181 is and to stop it leaving the States. Also, you are somehow to deliver it to the Embassy just like the last one. You will use no unnecessary violence and when you return here we will decide on your future.'

Francis Goddard placed both his hands face downwards on his desk side by side, it was a mannerism indicating a general reduction in the tension level and that the interview was nearing the end.

'Go and read up all the information

that Miller has — he's got all David's communications if you haven't seen them. Then check with Mrs Lorraine about your departure. There is unfortunately no one else I can send for over three weeks so I have no choice in this. Y181 must be kept from our friends at all costs — and you, it would appear in this particular instance, are the costs.'

Donahue tried to determine the meaning of the last remark as he rose to his feet sensing his instructions were complete.

'Marshall was one of the finest men I have ever known,' he said.

'I know that.'

'Anything else?'

'Luck.'

He left the deputy head with his hands still palms down on the white blotter beautifully covered with the decorative doodles which Goddard specialised in.

Donahue was in a very bad mood indeed. He had worked for Seven Nine, after becoming 'recruited' as they called it, for the last three years during which time he had become friends with David

Marshall. As far as he could tell, he had never, up until now, put a foot wrong with Goddard who was about as good a departmental head as you could get, so David had said. David had worked in Seven Nine ever since its formation twelve years ago, when the reclaiming of technical information from various foreign countries had become a frequent necessity. He had worked under five departmental chiefs and had repeatedly told Donahue that Goddard was one of the few that understood the lousy job that the field agents had.

Donahue had never before received anything but guidance from Goddard, never criticism and certainly never compliments. All previous mistakes had been taken apparently calmly and without rebuke, now after the recent blast from his chief, Donahue was surprised to find that he cared about his record.

He ran down the short flight of stairs to Colin Miller's office where all the records were kept, neatly filed under their project code names.

Soon he was sitting with a pile of

papers and files in front of him trying not to think of Jane, trying not to think of going back on assignment and trying not to care about what Goddard had said to him.

4

The State of Washington is a very large place. There is some desert, two mountain ranges, a great deal of magnificent forest and an endless shore line of silver grey sand. Except for the more frequented beaches, or those near the small coastal resort towns, the foreshores are almost universally covered with immense heaps of driftwood. Over the years, the rivers and the sea have taken the refuse of the logging industry, and together with the sun, the wind and the rain, have piled ton upon ton of twisted and bleached timber upon the dunes or stacked it against itself along the bases of the sloping shores.

Off shore, huge rocks protrude like the rotting teeth of a giant from the sea that froths eternally around them.

Wild lupins grow in profusion along the top of the grey crumbling shore on those stretches of coast where the trees allow sufficient light to reach the soil.

In summer, the great blue Pacific rolls wave after wave onto the sand rarely reaching the piles of silver and brown wood higher up the shore. On the larger beaches the surf can extend for nearly half a mile out to sea on a windy day, making it impossible to see the horizon from the beach.

At low tide beautiful sand dollars may be found lying on the flat wet sand, sometimes intact but more usually chipped or broken by the rough treatment previously received from the ocean.

It is a great pity that some of the more spectacular strips of coast cannot be visited by road, although this adds to the remoteness of those vast areas of shore. An experienced woodsman can fairly easily pack into these beaches from one of the dirt roads that lead into what is almost rain forest. Old Indian trails exist in a few places, some still covered with rough hewn planks laid sideways across the path to provide a solid footing.

As the years pass by, fewer and fewer

trails remain open, the great American nation preferring to visit the wilderness through the eye of the movie camera — helicopter borne at tree top height across the Washington woods.

The trek through humid undergrowth and virgin forest in the deep shade of the trees becomes very tiring unless you are either exceptionally fit or unless you are fortunate enough to be able to appreciate the environment for its unspoilt beauty.

There is one, or maybe two reasons why a man may be found camping alone near a game trail one and a half miles from the coast. The first would be hunting or trapping, the unlikely second would be hiding.

Simon Donahue was doing both.

Half way between a mirror-calm lake set deep in the woods on the Washington Olympic peninsula and Cape Alvera on the rock-strewn coast, the forest trail deteriorates suddenly. There is a small open clearing of coarse grass covering about ten acres in all, the kind that is called a prairie by local rangers. It is almost at the end of this prairie on the way to the sea that the trail changes from worn wooden slats buried in the peat and mud to a narrow track of nothing but slightly flattened grass smoothed by the passage of animals.

Donahue had bivouacked three hundred yards from the point where the trail changes its surface texture. The dark green one man tent of lightweight canvas was set in a shallow depression between three trees so that the ridge, which was no more than three and a half feet from the ground, was almost level with the surrounding terrain. In winter or even autumn, such a campsite would have been quite impossible. The Olympic peninsula has the highest rainfall of any area in the continental United States causing lichens to grow on every tree and bough and saturating the ground until it has the consistency of wet blotting paper.

The hollow that Donahue had chosen was not exactly dry despite it being July and that June, and so far all of July, had been completely rainless owing to some remarkable freak of Washington weather.

Although essentially very simple, the tiny ridge tent boasted two refinements, a thick waterproof floor, extending some four inches up each side of the walls, and a point — rather like the prow of a small boat — at the end opposite the entrance. It also had bug screens that could be zipped across the door.

In the pointed section, facing away from the trail, Donahue's rucksack stood with bulging pockets, while supported between the two tubular aluminium poles, hanging in the roof along the ridge was his bow. A quiver of arrows and a green silk sleeping bag completed the furnishing of the tent.

The files at Threadneedle Street had been little help. He had read each page twice, memorized as much detail of Y181 as he could and re-read copies of David Marshall's long transatlantic cables.

After thirteen hours flight to San Francisco by BOAC 707, he had on arrival immediately hired a 1500cc Volkswagen to drive the nine hundred miles up the winding coastal route to Seattle — the highway on which his friend had lost his life such a little while before.

A cable from Goddard had been waiting for him in California. One of the aircraft companies in San Francisco that had supplied parts to Guidance Systems Inc. had received an order for a replacement printed circuit board — identical to the previous two supplied for Y181. One of David Marshall's anonymous American friends had contacted Seven Nine in London mentioning the order from a box number in Washington State. The total information consisted purely of the box number at Midway Central Post Office.

Highway 101 is not a route for those in a hurry and Simon Donahue had taken his time, camping one night amongst the giant redwoods near the California-Oregon border.

During his trip north he had called again at the Oregon beach house which showed no further signs of habitation. In Tacoma, driving slowly past number eighty-seven Beachlands Avenue — the home of the late departed Ronald

Curtiss — Donahue had found he had no idea what he was looking for or what obscure reason prompted him to see the home of the man he had killed. He had found himself singularly unmoved by the experience apart from a rather guilty feeling that he was partially conforming to the accepted role of a murderer in visiting the home of his victim.

From Tacoma he had travelled directly to Midway where he enquired at the Post Office if it was possible for him to locate the owner of Box 18. He had not really expected a useful answer but nevertheless had been a little unprepared for the lecture received from an officious clerk concerning the sanctity of the US mail and the protection afforded to the lucky owners of Post Office boxes.

He had cabled Goddard informing him of his intentions and then settled down to wait.

For six days the white Volkswagen had parked outside the Post Office, and for six nights in the same place from the cramped confines of his car, Donahue had seen the same movie a mile away at the drive-in on the hill.

Luckily there were relatively few people keeping boxes at Midway Central Post Office. Donahue thought he knew most of them after three days of watching. His legs had cramped badly, ultimately his digestion had rejected the diet of hamburgers, hot dogs, and coke combined with a total lack of exercise and he had finally resolved that the sixth day would be the end of his vigil.

At 2.27 on July 27th an old but well kept Plymouth Fury had drawn up outside the Post Office. The driver, a burly man wearing extremely muddy boots and denim trousers, had disappeared into the building leaving the Plymouth blocking Donahue's vision from his carefully chosen strategic parking position. Quickly leaving the Volkswagen he had crossed the road in time to see the man juggling the key out of Box 18.

Donahue had seen other people enter the private box section of the Post Office many many times. On several previous occasions his view had been obscured but never before had he felt the impulse to leave the VW and check the customers box number. Perhaps it had been something about the dress of the man — or some sort of sixth sense; whatever it was, thankfully the long wait was over.

Whichever way you measure it — in cubic inches or in cc's — a Plymouth Fury has roughly four times the capacity of a Volkswagen in terms of engine size; the performance is in the same proportion.

From Midway out of the Seattle and Tacoma suburban sprawl, the drive across to the distant Olympics had been hectic for Donahue to say the least. It was essential that his white VW was not seen to be following the powerful American car — equally important, if Donahue's six day trial was not to be wasted, was that he did not lose it.

After several hours of rapid motoring the Plymouth had begun to leave the hard roads and take to the dirt. Following had become increasingly difficult without being detected although the distant dust cloud had proved to be a small help to the driver of the bouncing VW.

Eventually Donahue's map had shown him to be travelling on a dirt road leading to nowhere. The thin red line petered out on the map just as he imagined the road finally would.

He had stopped his pursuit, marked his map and returned to the Seattle motel where he had made his base on his earlier arrival in town. In view of the fact that no more than a few hours had been spent there during the six days, his bill had appeared a little surprising — however the Seven Nine expense account was almost a bottomless pit as far as Donahue was concerned and he paid the cheque almost cheerfully.

For the next few days he had busied himself in the big sporting goods stores downtown. There had been numerous problems in obtaining some of the more unusual commodities that were needed but eventually, through a friendly druggist who had spent some time trapping in British Columbia and understood the requirements, he was able to complete his kit.

Then, fully prepared, or so he hoped, Donahue had driven back to the peninsula, parked the VW in a small township and packed into the rain forest some two miles south of the old Alvera trail beneath the shadows of the great Olympic mountain range.

That had been nine days ago now.

For the first two days Donahue had done nothing but generally reconnoitre the country adjacent to the trail keeping a discreet distance from it where the scrub allowed. The hollow that he had selected for his bivouac was the best of a bad selection. Each side of the path through the forest was lined with broken rotting tree stumps and an almost impenetrable tangle of dense wet undergrowth prevented much in the way of excursion. He had not wanted to be out of earshot of the trail yet it was essential that his camp was quite hidden from sight. Finally the little hollow had been chosen as just about the only possible practical site — and there, on the third day, Donahue had set up his camp.

He had been prepared for a prolonged stay in the woods but Donahue knew that his supplies were limited especially with regard to water. A one ounce bottle of Halazone tablets purifies less water than you would imagine and he had been unable to obtain a larger quantity anywhere in Seattle. An additional ten iodine water purification tablets Donahue had brought with him as part of his normal supplies. These contain Tetraglycine Hydroperiodine and are principally intended for use in sub-tropical climates — Donahue hated the taste of water purified by iodine.

Food was not so much of a problem. There was an abundance of small game that he was able to kill silently with his long black arrows but he had never really been able to bring himself to enjoy uncooked meat.

Rather than resort to the iodine tablets he had toyed with the idea of lighting a fire in order to boil some of the brackish water, at the same time one of the rabbits could easily have been put on a green spit and barbecued. At night the embers of a small fire would be difficult to spot whilst the smoke would certainly have been undetected. Unfortunately the general dankness of the area could easily have retained a local pocket of smoke that would have lasted longer than Donahue would have wished.

And so, Simon Donahue had lived principally off the land for the last nine days, his cold raw food supplemented only by the few tins that he had packed in with him.

He had been relatively idle during this time.

The old Alvera trail leads directly to the Cape bearing the same name which has the doubtful distinction — if Alaska is excluded — of being the westernmost point of the United States.

Donahue had quickly found fresh mule tracks on the trail almost immediately after discovering the Plymouth parked at the end of the dirt road.

He had supposed that the previous occupants of the Oregon beach house

71

had moved to Cape Alvera for reasons best known to themselves — and at the moment quite unknown to him.

It was impossible for Donahue to use the trail. Firstly he could never be sure that he wouldn't run into someone round one of the many twists and bends through the trees: secondly he wished to avoid leaving his footprints on the muddy section in case they were to be later detected by an observant eye.

To his certain knowledge no one had passed either up or down the trail since his arrival, consequently it began to look as though he would have to proceed to the Cape while the man — or men — Donahue didn't know which, were still in residence. He had hoped that they would leave, at least temporarily, to obtain supplies; then after they had passed his bivouac on the trail he had intended to journey the one and a half miles to the coast for a rapid survey of the area.

There was some danger associated with such a manoeuvre inasmuch as Donahue was not sure how many men were currently at the Cape and anyway, he believed that it would be unlikely for them to leave their camp totally unguarded.

Even so, it might be possible, he thought, providing resistance was small, to remove the Y181 which he supposed was probably somewhere at the Cape.

On the night of the ninth day, now thoroughly fed up with waiting — especially after his previous six days in the Volkswagen, Donahue decided he would move.

Movement, other than in daylight, was impossible either on the trail or through the bush. He resolved that he would use the trail starting at first light on the following morning.

As the men had not used the main access to the Cape for at least nine days Donahue was worried that he would find nothing on arrival. It was quite possible that the Y181, if it had ever been there, was now either miles out to sea or someway up the coast by now. Why the coast of the Pacific North West had been apparently chosen as a temporary home for the sunseeker he could not imagine.

Goddard had mentioned the impossibility of shipping anything as delicate and large as Y181 by usual undercover means, he had also said that there was no definite evidence to indicate that it was to be shipped anywhere.

All Donahue could do was to approach the Cape as warily as possible to a point where he could find out exactly what was happening there — providing that something was happening and providing that he was not too late.

Before dark, Donahue prepared his kit in readiness for the following morning. He laid out his binoculars, his knife and sufficient food for two days. The leather bush jacket he would wear had two long tubes sewn into the outside of the back vertically up the spine. Into these he slid his special arrows while the food and his water flask he buttoned into the pockets. Map, compass and medical kit were also contained in individually tailored compartments in the jacket sides and front.

As the last Stellars Jay fluttered noisily from the hollow to roost for the night,

Donahue ate a frugal meal of pemmican and raw wild horsetail shoots washed down with a cup of sterile water in which four squares of Horlicks had been dissolved.

Then, glad that he had decided on action at last, he slid into his sleeping bag and listened to the crickets singing to each other in the deepening dusk outside the tent.

5

He woke whilst it was still dark. Nothing could be seen through the gauze of the fly screen stretched tightly across the front of the tent.

It was raining.

In the wet season the rain is not torrential, rather there is a continuous drizzle for days or weeks on end, sometimes interrupted by heavier downpours. In the summer the rain is much more sporadic but very heavy.

This morning, by the sound of the drops pattering on the walls of the tent, a gentle rain was falling. Donahue hoped that it would either stop or at worst continue at its present moderate rate — if it turned into a typical storm he was going to get very wet indeed.

The sleeping bag was warm and snug, its protective comfort spoilt only by the tab on the zip lying cold on his cheek.

Donahue lit a cigarette.

There was no point in attempting to leave until there was sufficient light for him to see the trail easily and this morning would be darker than usual. He knew from experience that he would want no breakfast. The inside of the tent was damp, the air moist and the cigarette smoke seemed reluctant to filter away through the fly screen — you couldn't smoke for long with your head at the closed end of such a tiny tent.

For perhaps half an hour he lay listening to the steady rain. If it continued for long, Donahue's forest hollow would become a swamp. Already the shallow groove he had scooped out of the ground for his hip began to feel cold through the sleeping bag.

He was not particularly depressed at the change of weather — it was rare for weather conditions to be ideal on assignment. Invariably it seemed the days were too hot, too wet, or too cold, whilst the nights either had too much or too little moonlight for comfort.

Like a snake shedding an old skin, Donahue slid out of the warmth of his bed. Lying on his back he added the few clothes that would be necessary for his trip to the Cape. Apart from footwear, he was almost fully dressed already. Donahue had no space, no time and no inclination to use night clothes. Although just able to struggle into the leather bush jacket he could not sit up in the little tent to pull on the waterproof lace up boots.

Donahue wriggled worm-like out of the tent after unzipping the screen at the entrance with his feet. Standing on one foot feeling the wet seep immediately through his woollen sock he quickly slipped on the boots.

It was still dark.

From the tent ridge he withdrew his black bow and strung it. Laminated wooden bows might be sweeter and have a better cast, in weather like this there was no substitute whatever for a completely durable glass fibre stave. Donahue thought of the 15th century English archers who kept their bow strings dry by wrapping them next to their bodies beneath their jerkins. A dacron string would have been worth a small fortune in those distant years. There had been little surprise associated with the chivalrous battles that had raged across the face of medieval Europe and there had been no need for the English to have their bows strung until a moment before combat. Donahue thought that it would be nice to know exactly when you would need to use your bow.

Perhaps he should have brought the hand-gun, the Ruger Blackhawk .44 magnum with the long silencer. His instructions of 'no unnecessary violence' were much easier to follow using only his bow and knife when compared with the instant death that a gun could provide.

Almost automatically he had begun to walk westward along the trail as soon as the watery dawn allowed the outline of the muddy puddled track to be seen against the background of forest mirk.

It was easier to move quietly on wet ground with no dry twigs to snap and no leaves to rustle. Donahue made good time. The nine day wait had convinced him that the chance of meeting the opposition on the trail was remote, and at first light on a wet morning he felt that extreme caution was not necessary.

In less than half an hour Donahue could sense that the coast was near. Although the light had been increasing steadily, despite the very low cloud, some extra quality that seashores have the world over, told him that the Pacific was only a few turns of the trail away.

Beautiful though the Alvera trail may be, on a wet July morning a good deal of the charm is lost. It was certainly lost to Simon Donahue who had progressively tensed as the trail began to open out. Now, as he stood on a small rise on the edge of the trees looking seawards across a narrow strip of grass, the familiar churning in his stomach began.

The beach was very rocky. A quarter of a mile out to sea an island rose splendidly from the grey water. Shaped rather like a Gothic arch, almost unbelievably symmetrical with a small flat plateau on the top it was perhaps 300 feet high. The tide was out giving Donahue the impression that you could wade easily through shallow water to the base of the island if you wanted to. He thought that he would very much like to bring Jane here one hot sunny day — just the two of them alone with the wildness of the rocks and water. One day soon.

Across the grass in front of him, to the right of a natural line drawn between the end of the trail and the sea, stood a crude shack of silvered cedar.

The building was not the efforts of an early homesteader or trapper. Donahue knew exactly what it was.

All along the Pacific North West Coast, American Indians had built temporary shelters long long ago. Tribes would migrate north and south, staying for months at a time in one particular place where they would gather shellfish and hunt the deer and elk. Then, tiring of their camp, the instinctive wanderers would move on to greener pastures. Behind them, at their campsites, enormous heaps of clam shells have accumulated over the years and in some especially choice locations small 'A' frame lean-to dwellings have been built.

The American Government have allowed some of the more established sites to remain the property of the now almost extinct Indian tribes. By law, in order to retain their rights, these sites have to be occupied for at least one day per year. For decades, it has been rare for this regulation to be enforced, and even rarer for the elders of the tribes to bother to uphold their rights.

In the grey morning drizzle Donahue looked at the Alvera Indian camp wondering if the little rickety cabin was occupied at the moment.

As it was still early it was unlikely that anyone would be up and about and there was no way to tell whether or not the cabin was being used. Donahue had no recourse but to settle down and wait; a part he was becoming accustomed to playing on this assignment.

The leather of his jacket was saturated with water but nevertheless had prevented the upper part of his body from becoming wet so far — the same could not be said of his jeans. Rain had rapidly soaked through to his legs, running down to his ankles to be slowly absorbed by the thick woollen socks he wore. Waterproof boots certainly prevented his feet from becoming wet if he stepped in a puddle — they were no use at all under present conditions.

Donahue reckoned the temperature was around seventy degrees already so the general wetness of his skin and clothing did not bother him unduly. Once the initial unpleasantness of actually feeling the water seep through his jeans was over he had become used to the dampness from his waist down.

He stepped out from the cover of the trees walking quietly and carefully towards a tangle of scrub one third of the way across the clearing. He kept a wary eye out for the thin wires that so easily could be stretched across a field at ankle height.

There was not much more detail to be seen of the cabin as Donahue approached the scrub.

Cracks between the planks forming the sides gave the whole structure such a ramshackle appearance that he doubted if it was fit for habitation. Earlier he had used his binoculars to obtain a better view of the unique island and to check the surrounding area of beach for signs of a camp. Now he started to withdraw them again from one of his big front pockets, intending to take a further look at the cabin, now seeming to be the only possible place where anyone could be based.

They stuck against the wet leather.

Still walking forward but looking down transiently at the binoculars now almost free, Donahue collided gently with a young sapling growing on the edge of the scrub outcrop.

The air was rent with a violent noise.

It sounded like a circular saw screaming through a green log.

He dropped to the ground behind the small patch of undergrowth, his heart leaping in his chest. The eerieness of the sound, so unexpected and so loud had frightened Simon Donahue very much indeed.

His fear vanished in a matter of seconds

as his brain identified the noise.

The damned burro or donkey.

This morning the light had been inadequate and the trail too muddy for Donahue to determine either footprints or mule shoe marks. He had not forgotten the animal but had quite obviously neglected to consider its presence more seriously.

Apparently it was tethered to a part of the bush that he was crouched behind and it was terribly frightened.

The bush shook while the burro continued to make the most indescribable noise.

Donahue had but one sensible course of action.

A quick glance at the cabin and he was running fast across the clearing to the cover of the trees.

Less than two seconds after he had moved there was a 'crack' behind him.

Mud spurted beside the heel of his left foot.

Now Donahue knew.

He began to zig-zag — only a few yards more.

The calf of his right leg exploded in searing pain.

Donahue, almost within touching distance of the dense cover of the trees fell hard and flat on his face from his headlong run.

His leg felt as though it were immersed up to the knee in molten steel.

He sat up, rolled over and drew an arrow from over his shoulder.

In a trice the nock was on the string between the two bumps of red silk binding.

Nearly blinded from the pain in his leg and with hands covered in mud after the fall, Donahue vainly attempted to draw the sixty pound bow. He had to hold the weapon awkwardly in a horizontal position in order to clear the ground with the bow tips.

He couldn't make it.

Two men were running towards him from the cabin.

One stopped at the sight of Donahue attempting to pull on the bow and the other dropped to the ground and levelled a rifle.

Knowing there was no hope now Donahue dropped the useless weapon and threw himself back on the grass.

There was no bullet.

No bullet biting its way up through his crotch into his belly.

The pain in his calf spread upwards. Donahue was paralysed by the awfulness of it.

He could think of nothing but the pain.

Filmily he saw a man appear on each side of him and from the corner of his eye saw the rifle butt move.

His head burst in a shower of red and green flashing columns of light.

★ ★ ★

A black shutter repeatedly allowed a thin line of light to shine in his eyes as it lifted. In his right temple the pain was so intense when the shutter rose that Donahue had successfully wished it shut again at least four times.

This time it didn't work. Up and up it went.

He screwed his eyes shut but it made no difference — painfully the light increased in intensity as the shutter opened wider.

His head pounded unbearably. Donahue thought the pressure would burst his forehead apart.

Surprised that the pain did not increase still further he opened his eyes very slightly and squinted beneath his eyelids.

There were no stars to vanish when he looked at them, no flashing lights, no red haze.

Very slowly Donahue oriented himself with his surroundings. He was lying on his side on a bare earth floor looking up at a rough table made from splintered planks.

From experience he carefully avoided moving his head knowing that the shutter would descend once more leaving him with the unpleasant job of regaining consciousness all over again.

Through the thickness of the throbbing Donahue began to try and remember. Then, as the earlier events of the morning were recalled he slowly moved his head over the soil until he could see his legs.

He was lying on his right side. The throbbing was awful as soon as he moved. More awful was the sight of his right leg. From his ankle to half way up his thigh, his jeans were stained with blood. The earth beneath his leg was red, so was his right sock — all a thin watery red.

It didn't hurt.

He wondered how much blood he had lost and how long he had been lying in the cabin. He remembered the blow on his head and the pain from the bullet in his leg but Donahue had absolutely no idea how long ago it all had happened. It was essential for him to find out the extent of the injury to his leg.

He rolled over onto his back fighting the bursting pressure in his temples. Then, still very slowly, he began to push himself into a sitting position using his arms as props.

When his trunk was vertical Donahue began to draw up his knees — still no pain from the leg. Now he could see that the red stain soaked into the denim of his jeans was not pure blood — the material, already saturated by the rain had dispersed the blood from the wound until now a uniform thin red solution had been formed. It was obviously not as bad as it looked.

He felt for his knife.

Surprisingly it was still at his belt.

Donahue slit the wet jeans sawing upwards from the ankle trying at intervals in vain to tear the heavy fabric. When he reached the knee he was able to feel round behind his leg to the fleshy part of the calf. It was very swollen and there seemed to be a small hole each side of the muscle. The leg was quite numb. He thought that the bullet might with luck have passed right through, maybe glancing off the bone in the centre.

He had been shot twice before — on both occasions he had suffered flesh wounds which seemed to have been relatively painless compared with this one. He didn't think the bone was broken.

It would be a good trick if he could stand up, providing head and leg could stand it.

Using the table as a steady, Donahue

pulled himself painfully to his feet taking care to avoid placing any weight on his right leg. It began to ache and beads of blood appeared at the entry and exit punctures of the wound as he tried to shift his position.

Propped up against the table Donahue looked around him. The pain in his head no longer caused him to fear a lapse into unconsciousness. He was nearly convinced that his ideas on the nature of his leg wound were correct and he felt that there was hope yet.

The cabin was a good deal larger inside than he expected — rather like a large tent in shape with a few rudimentary struts of wood bracing the sides where the planks were especially weak or bent. Two camp beds stood side by side at one of the triangular ends. In the centre of the room there was a propane cooker surrounded by an untidy stack of empty food cans.

He was leaning against one of the benches or tables which ran the length of each sloping wall.

Several metal cases — the precise

function of which Donahue could only guess at — stood on the benches, all of them covered with transparent polythene to protect them from the drops of rain seeping through the numerous cracks and holes in the building. Condensation prevented a clear view of the equipment underneath the plastic but he could see enough to know he was looking at electronic test equipment of some kind.

Donahue wondered if Y181 was in the cabin.

He had a sudden wild idea of smashing up everything in sight. He probably had the strength to do a pretty thorough job even though it would take some time.

Any such action would have been short-lived. The noise would certainly attract the owners of the expensive equipment layed out under the protective covering of polythene — they would not be far away Donahue thought — not to leave him alone in the cabin even though he had been unconscious.

Smashing the equipment would not enhance his chances of survival. These men had already shown a good deal of ruthlessness in arranging David Marshall's death a month ago — if not actually killing him themselves. They would not be men to trifle with.

Y181 was not as important to Donahue as his life. Already, he assessed his position as being one of little hope; while he was alive there was always a chance for survival and perhaps to do something about the sunseeker. He was not yet ready to sacrifice himself for the sake of a piece of guidance electronics.

There was nothing on the benches that looked like Y181 from the photographs that Donahue had seen in London, rather the equipment was commercial laboratory gear — some of it appearing to be partially packed in new cardboard cartons. He doubted if it was being used in the cabin. A Coleman white gas hurricane lantern hung in the roof and nowhere was there evidence of any portable electrical generator.

Now his leg was beginning to hurt more, but the pain in his head was diminishing gradually, allowing Donahue to think more clearly.

He still had his knife clutched in a bloody hand, he could walk — just, and he was alive. Donahue thought things could have been a lot worse.

What a fool he'd been to have forgotten the burro — nine days wait in the forest for nothing — to blow the whole thing by running into a burro — he didn't deserve to be alive.

Edging his way gingerly to a clear area on the bench he levered himself up until he was sitting on the boards. Taking the weight off his leg was not as successful at reducing the pain as he expected — he wanted to lie down.

Donahue had scarcely begun to think of what he should do when voices outside announced the return of his captors.

The door of the cabin opened.

6

He barely had time to thrust his knife into his pocket before two men ducked their way through the low door.

They stared at Donahue.

With considerable effort he managed a grin.

Had he been able to see himself he would probably not have bothered. One side of his head was streaked with dried blood, the torn leg of his jeans, a watery red, flapped in the draught from the open door and his clothes were smeared with thick patches of mud.

The first man into the cabin — the larger of the two, was the one Donahue had followed from Midway Post Office. The second he had never seen before.

Both were wearing black plastic rain-coats.

The smaller man was carrying Donahue's arrow in one hand and a rifle in the other.

They stood side by side along the end wall looking silently at the man sitting on the bench.

Donahue said. 'Hi.'

'Who are you?' the small man spoke.

'Simon Donahue, I was hunting — fell over your bloody burro just before you shot me.'

The small man took off his raincoat and hung it up.

'You don't seriously expect us to believe you, Mr Donahue.'

'Believe what you like — I want a doctor for my leg and an explanation from you.'

The man smiled. From his speech he was a North American but from what part Donahue was not able to tell.

'Mr Donahue, you're lucky to be alive — very lucky. I shot you in the leg, I could just as easily have shot you in the stomach. I haven't any idea how you found your way to Cape Alvera although I'm sure your presence here is not accidental. I am also sure that you have meddled in our affairs before. I refer to the death of one Ronald Curtiss who — ' the man raised the hand holding Donahue's arrow, 'was killed with a hunting arrow some days ago. It's pointless for you to pretend that you're not here by design and I suggest that you stop being stupid.'

Donahue thought that his current position was not the best. His bow had been an obvious link with Curtiss. Did they suspect that David Marshall had been connected with Donahue?

He remained silent.

The larger man moved forward to the propane cooker and lit the burner. From a large screw top jar he shook some instant coffee into two metal cups and an empty fruit juice can.

While the water was heating the two men removed their heavy boots and dried the rain from their faces and hair.

They said nothing to each other or to Donahue.

Soon, Donahue was drinking hot coffee from the juice can wondering what the next move was to be.

The small man spoke again.

'Mr Donahue, we've already been

bothered by one Englishman — a Mr David Marshall — he's dead. Despite your accent I'm sure you're English too and that for us to have had the misfortune to have been interrupted in our work by two Englishmen is more than a coincidence. Marshall was not particularly helpful or forthcoming before he died, nevertheless we've got enough information to know that the British are anxious to recover all the data of the Astra Physics Y181 sunseeker. In this cabin we have a Y181 and a case of microfilmed drawings. These will shortly be used to good effect to further the cause of the great Soviet Republic. You are too late I'm afraid, much too late.'

The man spoke quickly with sudden hand movements. He was a uniformly small man, hardly taller than five feet with a well balanced frame. An air of confidence was apparent in the way he addressed Donahue.

His colleague had remained silent since entering the cabin. Now he put down his empty cup on the bench and walked to where Donahue was sitting. He was as large as the other was small.

'Smoke?'

Donahue gratefully took a cigarette from the proffered packet watching the eyes of the man as he leant forward for the light.

The big man was nervous. His hands shook a little as he held the match. Donahue wondered why.

Again the small man addressed him.

'If you'd arrived tomorrow you'd have found nothing, you would still have failed in your mission but you would not be going to die.'

His expression changed.

'We've a hell of a lot of work to do to-day — tie him up Chuck, put him on the floor and let's get on with the packing.'

Donahue let the big man tie his wrists.

'I can keep out of the way, don't tie my ankles, the leg hurts like hell.'

Chuck looked at the small man for guidance.

'That's OK, help him over to the far corner — he can't hurt anything.'

Donahue had contributed nothing of

consequence so far to the conversation. He had not been asked to, which was perfectly OK by him. The reference to his impending death was not made in a way designed to horrify, rather it was a plain statement of fact completely devoid of emotion. It had not really frightened Donahue. He had not expected anything else.

Now, as he sat on the earth floor leaning against the end wall, he tried to establish some sort of plan. The coffee had helped his head enormously whilst the wound in his leg, now no longer seeping blood, was almost bearable. He could still not have moved without the help of the big man Chuck, but at least they had not tied his legs together before dumping him on the floor.

Both men busied themselves about the cabin, sealing the electronic units into cardboard cartons with masking tape. Each box was placed in a polythene bag the mouths of which were welded tightly together using a metal rod heated over the little propane stove.

In all there were nine boxes, all of

varying size. Some had been already packaged prior to Donahue's arrival and, as he had still not seen anything looking like Y181, he assumed that the unit must be in one of the cartons, the contents of which he had been unable to see.

He was totally ignored as the men worked.

After nearly four hours Donahue received more coffee and half a can of warm soup. His hands were untied while he drank.

He had to ask.

'What's the deal?'

'You've been wondering I'm sure.'

Donahue had no plan and had become despondent about his inability to move under his own steam; he could do absolutely nothing.

The small man smiled pleasantly.

'This afternoon we get our final instructions. At that time I'll ask if you're to be dealt with here or if we're to take you with us for interrogation. Either way, Mr Donahue time is short.'

Everything was said without malice in

an almost incongruously cheerful manner, seemingly with complete disinterest.

Donahue's leg had stopped being numb. Now the pain was severe again, localized in the area of the bullet wound — it seemed to come in spasms.

He felt very tired.

Without knowing, mentally and physically spent from his fight against the pain, he fell into a fatigued sleep.

The bang of the cabin door woke him.

His ankles were tied now as well as his hands.

'Ah, Mr Donahue.'

The small man waved his hand at the trussed body on the floor.

'You are to come with us to the *Vertaz*.'

'Where?'

'The ship — the *Vertaz*.'

Donahue saw the transmitter hanging by a leather strap from the shoulder of the big man called Chuck.

'When?'

'When the tide is high enough.'

Donahue thought that the *Vertaz* must

be a very small ship if she was to come into the Cape.

The two men began to carry the boxes out of the cabin. It had stopped raining, the low cloud had gone and a late afternoon watery sun was raising mist from the ground outside the door. Donahue could see the mist each time the door opened; he wished he could be outside in the sun for a while — for the last time.

Soon the cabin was empty apart from the pile of empty cans and the man lying on the floor.

Donahue's watch had stopped. It was nearly four o'clock he guessed, about high tide when he heard the outboard.

The drone was very faint but increasing steadily in volume. It must have been half an hour later that the noise stopped at the beach leaving an empty silence in the cabin.

Chuck appeared at the door.

'Come on, it's time.'

Except for one or two words while they were packing and the time that he had offered Donahue a cigarette he had not

103

spoken. The merest trace of an accent could be detected, not American yet not European.

The nylon cord was removed from Donahue's ankles letting him move slowly and painfully using Chuck as a giant crutch.

Once outside the cabin there might be a chance.

A chance to do what — he thought bitterly. What the hell could he do. If they left him at the Cape it would be doubtful if he would survive in his present condition, anyway they wouldn't leave him alive.

Donahue saw the burro.

The small man was untying its halter from the bush. He patted the animal which walked slowly across the clearing, ears pricked, looking at the activity on the beach.

A large launch with twin Evinrude outboard motors floated on the calm water about a hundred yards from the water's edge. Two strangers Donahue had not seen before, presumably they had arrived with the launch, were wading to the shore where the pile of boxes stood.

He thought again of Jane.

It was still a beautiful place. Even in the rain he had known that Cape Alvera would look the way it did now in the sunshine.

Jane. He knew all along that one day it would happen. Was this the time?

'How about a cigarette?' he asked.

Donahue leant against Chuck while the man fumbled for the pack. This time the hand holding the match didn't shake.

Looking over his shoulder greedily at the forest behind him for the last time, Donahue resumed his slow journey to the beach.

'I'll carry you if you want, but the salt water might do the leg some good.' Chuck said gruffly.

'What's the point if you're going to kill me?'

Donahue felt strangely churlish. The big man had not been unkind — in fact neither man had attempted to be anything but reasonable since his capture.

'No it's OK, I'll walk, give me a hand.'

Donahue, still leaning heavily against the shoulder of his warder started to paddle.

The salt water was acid — pouring into his leg from both sides at once. Sweat poured off Donahue stumbling on his one good leg over slippery submerged rocks and stones. Although the pain slowly abated as he waded, after eighty yards the water was waist high and he was physically finished.

Chuck, sensing that the injured man was close to his limit lifted him easily over his shoulder and pushed his way through the last remaining twenty yards of sea.

At the boat he tipped Donahue over the gunwale leaving him like a sack of wheat, half in and half out. Chuck climbed over the port side and pulled the helpless man onto a seat in the stern.

The warmth of the sun started to dry out Donahue's clothes, it was hotter than it had appeared through the cabin door. By the time all the boxes had been stowed and all the men were on board, he was feeling better again.

The roar of the motors echoed across the Cape bouncing off the little island now completely surrounded by relatively deep water.

Donahue watched the island recede as the boat sped seawards. His hands had been tied again with the ends of the nylon securely knotted to a handy cleat. He wondered if they thought he might jump overboard.

Ahead of them the late afternoon sun shone through the foam-flecked windscreen so that Donahue could see nothing from his seat in the rear. He watched the Washington shore line fall behind the white wake — would he ever see it again, see Jane, Goddard and all the others; he had almost given up already.

Night was creeping across the Pacific by the time the engines were throttled back. Donahue could see the large vessel ahead of them floating motionless on the oily water. As the launch came alongside, two coils of heavy manilla rope were thrown down. These were quickly attached to special eyelets fitted fore and aft on the deck and in a matter of moments the ropes tightened as the chattering donkey engine above them began to take the strain.

When the keel of the launch was above the rail of the rusty deck of the ship, davits swung the cargo inboard. Soon the launch was secured in a cradle on the deck plates and Russian sailors were swarming round them on all sides.

Donahue was lifted out roughly and dropped on a stretcher. He was taken below to an extremely tiny cabin with a single dirty porthole where the handles of the stretcher were placed on wooden crates — one at each end.

He had only time to sit up before the steel door clanged shut. Simultaneously vibration started through the hull as the screws began to turn.

The *Vertaz* was underway.

On deck the boxes were being unloaded from the launch, sailors carrying them below under the instruction of a junior officer. The big parabolic radar reflectors rotated lazily on the superstructure of the fishing vessel like the blades of a fan as the Russian spy ship steamed away from the west coast of the United States. She had been there too close too long and the captain wanted to put a respectable distance between him and the coast by morning; also he was three hours behind schedule which must be made up as quickly as possible.

In his cabin Donahue peered out at the dark through the porthole. He could see absolutely nothing.

After he had resigned himself to the fact that he was now the prisoner of the Communists, being shipped to an unknown destination for an unknown purpose, he started to wonder about the interrogation the small man had mentioned.

He knew little about Y181 which could be good or bad depending on the questions. If they knew about Seven Nine the questions might be very searching and impossible for him to answer — again Donahue could do nothing but wait.

His wait was not to last long.

The scraping of the stiff catch against the rusty door showed that he was not to be left to his own devices.

An officer and the little man from the Cape entered the room.

The officer spoke in Russian — apparently a question. Both chatted for a moment with an occasional glance at the Englishman. The small man can't be an American after all, Donahue thought, not unless he could speak fluent Russian.

'You are Simon Donahue?' the officer spoke in passable English.

'Yes.'

'You are from the British Seven Nine organization?'

Donahue looked blank.

'Seven Nine in London.'

They know — they know, damn them. Donahue felt the sweat break out beneath his arms. He said nothing.

'What have you got to do with Y181?'

Donahue shrugged 'I haven't any idea what you're talking about.'

The officer looked at him for an instant then swiftly kicked Donahue's leg with the shiny toe of his shoe.

Donahue had been sitting on the stretcher during the interview. He had seen the kick coming but could not drag his injured leg out of the way in time.

He bent double clutching the calf of his leg with both hands as waves of pain rolled from toe to hip.

'I am an officer on the *Vertaz*, it is not my job to make you talk. That can wait. If you are no trouble you will be kept here until we return, then they can do what they like with you.'

Donahue hadn't understood what the man had said. Blood was pouring down his leg and he felt faint.

'Pig English.' The officer spat on the back of Donahue's neck as the wounded man sat hunched on the stretcher nursing his leg.

The door of the prison shut.

Simon Donahue lifted his leg up onto the stretcher and turned over onto his stomach.

He punched the canvas with his fist, sobbing with a mixture of exasperation, self-pity and pain.

An hour later a sailor entered the cabin carrying a tray which he placed on the floor.

'Lavatory, toilet,' Donahue said.

The sailor looked puzzled.

Donahue pretended to unzip his fly.

The sailor grinned and went out.

He returned shortly with a plastic bucket. He pointed to the porthole and made an emptying motion.

Donahue nodded.

Until the tray had been brought he hadn't really felt hungry but now the sight of food made him realize that he was. Since leaving camp in the morning he had only drunk two cups of black coffee and half a can of soup. If he was to regain his strength he would have to eat and he attacked the meal of coarse brown bread, vegetables and meat as though he had not eaten for a week.

When the sailor reappeared to take away the tray, Donahue used sign language to ask for a cigarette. The sailor gave him a packet of Russian ones and a half empty book of matches.

After the food and a cigarette, Donahue curled up on the stretcher resting his head on his arm. Then, making his mind a blank and attempting to forget his wretched leg, he tried to rest.

The throb of engines and the fatigue caused by the day's events soon sent Simon Donahue thankfully into a deep sleep.

The *Vertaz* with lights set cut its way through the dark sea moving on to its next rendezvous. In a long air-conditioned cabin immediately below Donahue's, three Russian electronic engineers were looking at the mass of wiring and electro-mechanics that was Y181.

7

He was still asleep when the clang of the cabin door announced the entry of the seaman who had brought his meal the night before. It was daylight and the porthole allowed a circular column of sunlight to shine on the dirty whitewashed wall of Donahue's tiny cell.

The Russian placed a wooden tray on the floor and muttered something that Donahue could not understand. Receiving no answer, the man shrugged and left the cabin.

Very gently, Donahue swung both legs off the hammock placing his feet carefully on the floor. The steel buzzed through the soles of his boots with engine vibration.

His leg was a peculiar blue colour from the knee down and totally insensitive to the pressure of Donahue's exploring hand. He didn't like the look of it at all.

His clothes were almost completely

dry, and he judged that the temperature in the room was over eighty degrees.

On the breakfast tray stood an enormous white enamel mug containing black coffee, two thick brown sandwiches filled with what appeared to be a type of sausage meat and an apple. Donahue thought the apple looked very much out of place.

He was surprisingly hungry and easily managed to swallow most of both sandwiches with the aid of copious draughts of hot sweet coffee.

He lit a cigarette and began to think seriously of the position he was in.

When the man returned to collect the tray, Donahue pointed to his leg and said. 'Doctor.'

As there was no sign of understanding it was with some surprise that Donahue greeted the subsequent arrival of the ship's doctor a few minutes later.

The doctor was quick, efficient and, as far as Donahue was concerned, totally unsympathetic. His wound was prodded from all directions and his calf squeezed and pushed. It seemed that the bullet had passed right through as Donahue had suspected. After swabbing his leg and pouring a quantity of powder into each side of the puncture, the doctor bound it comfortably in a substantial length of stiff white bandage. Two injections, both in Donahue's left arm, and the treatment was over. The doctor left without having said a word from the beginning to the end of his visit.

Alone once again, Donahue stood up, propping himself against the wall of the cabin. He peered through the grime of the porthole but could see nothing except the dark green sea below stretching flatly through the dusk to the limit of his vision.

He had no idea whatever where he was going or even why he was being taken, apart from the remarks of the officer when he had first been brought on board the *Vertaz*.

Escape was virtually impossible. At best he could jump over the side but there was certainly little point in that and it would accomplish nothing. The chances of taking over control of the

Vertaz were so small as to be laughable but Donahue could think of no other solution. There was no alternative but to wait for his captors to make the next move.

He waited for three days.

On the morning of the fourth day of his confinement, the officer who had kicked his leg accompanied the seaman who brought breakfast.

Donahue felt his body tense a little.

'How long are you going to keep me in this damn cabin?' Donahue spoke through a mouthful of sour sausage sandwich.

The officer leaned against the door whilst Donahue ate.

'How long?'

'You are to come with me now.' The guttural English lisped out between fat lips.

Donahue rose from his stretcher hammock and limped through the door held open by the officer with exaggerated politeness.

By now the leg had improved a good deal as a result of three days enforced rest. On the second day the doctor had briefly re-appeared and inspected Donahue's wound. On leaving he had smiled slightly at his patient and said, 'OK.' in a hesitant but pleasant voice.

Sensing the presence of the officer behind him, Donahue walked stiffly down a long dimly lit corridor with closed steel doors evenly spaced on each wall. Seemingly it lead nowhere, but at the end was a steel ladder, rungs and hand-rails polished smooth by the action of shoes and hands.

He half turned; the officer waving him on up the steps.

A small landing at the top was the terminal for other similar corridors, presumably on the deck above the one on which he had been imprisoned.

Roughly pushing past, the Russian walked some twenty feet down the nearest passage and opened one of the doors.

Donahue followed and entered a small wood-panelled room.

Two people awaited him.

One was the small man from the Cape,

the other — a typical figure of a Russian who Donahue had not seen before.

The officer, who had come in behind, said something in Russian. The stranger answered sharply causing the man to retreat — closing the door quietly behind him.

The small man smiled pleasantly. 'Please sit down, Mr Donahue.'

Donahue sat on a small leather chair looking warily at the two men and wondering about the reason for the summons.

'We are now nearly one thousand miles from the west coast of the United States. As you have been shut up in your cabin for several days, it occurred to us that you would perhaps like to talk — or rather to listen for a while.'

Donahue wondered what the last remark was intended to convey.

He said, 'Thank you for sending the doctor,' and stopped abruptly wondering what else was expected.

'Are you not going to ask us any questions?' The small man spoke again.

It had never occurred to Donahue

that he would have the opportunity to ask questions. Almost automatically he had simply assumed that Y181 would be taken to Russia for evaluation and for copying whilst he would go for the usual interrogation.

'What do you mean?' he asked.

'Mr Donahue, I am disappointed in you. You are neither dull nor stupid and in fact came surprisingly near to upsetting our plans. Your Seven Nine organization is to be congratulated on their choice of agent. However, I am sure that you cannot believe that we have gone to this much trouble just to obtain a prototype of Y181 to take back to the USSR. If that had been our only intention we could easily have sent the microfilms to our Institute of Automation and Telemechanics in Moscow where we would have busied ourselves with reproducing your design to the best of our ability.'

The man stood up from the brown leather-covered bench that he had been sitting on and waved a hand at his colleague still staring at Donahue.

'This is Professor Petrov of the State Committee of Science and Technology at Cazazhstan. The professor has been controller of a rather unusual but important project for the past two and one half years. Forgetting that for a moment — you will be interested to learn that the Soviet Republic will, within the next eighteen months launch the nucleus of the first manned orbital satellite sub-station — an adaption of our successful Soyuz space vehicle. After adding progressively to this station, which will earth orbit at an altitude of about 500 kilometres, it will be used as a base for deep space manned probes and also for military surveillance purposes.'

Donahue remained passive, listening intently to the little Russian pacing slowly round the confines of the cabin, occasionally waving a hand at the professor to emphasize a particularly important point.

'Until that time, it is important for my country to preserve the world image of technological success that we have so carefully built over the past few years.

Y181 is required for two reasons; firstly it may prove to be superior to our own stable platform system to be used in the satellite station, and secondly, because it is essential to Professor Petrov's project.'

The professor nodded and lit a cigarette.

Donahue suddenly realized that the professor must be able to speak, or at least understand English. Simon Donahue was very interested in Professor Petrov.

The small man continued.

'Like you, we in the Soviet Union cannot yet produce optical encoders to the necessary accuracy. This was one of the reasons that we chose to produce the two Y181 units in America. The other reason was speed.

One Y181 — the only one we have — will be used in a matter of a few days; we could not, I regret, have produced one so quickly as we have done without the help of the Americans.

You already know that two prototypes have been manufactured using as far as possible our own components. I may say our development in that direction is encouraging — however there still remains a large amount of work to be done before Y181 can even be considered for the satellite.'

The professor spoke. 'You understand all this, Mr Donahue?' There was a hint of a sneer in the voice.

Donahue nodded. 'Yes, I understand perfectly.'

The small man sat down suddenly. 'Please allow me to continue,' he said.

Donahue lit the last cigarette from the packet the sailor had given him. He said nothing.

The little Russian began again. 'The single Y181 that is on board this ship is, as I speak, being prepared by our engineers for a most important task. Soon, it will be transferred to one of our nuclear missile-carrying submarines where it will be fitted to a new very high-altitude missile of the FOBS type — that is one of our Fractional Orbital Bombardment vehicles. This will be launched exactly four days from now from a point in the central Pacific Ocean. After blast off, and once in orbit, Y181 will be used to orient the missile precisely into a very particular precalculated position. Incidentally the sunseeker will of course serve a very similar purpose in our sub-station in some months time.

'At mid-day on July 14th the missile will be reactivated and will use an ordinary infrared homing system to establish a collision course with another space vehicle that will be entering the earth's atmosphere at that time.'

Donahue became alert.

'I have already mentioned the necessity for our country to remain, in the eyes of the world at least, on a similar technological level to your American friends. When we launch our orbital station of course it is obvious that Soviet prestige will soar ahead. Until that time, our politicians have considered it wise to make sure that the NASA Space Programme suffers certain failures.

'To this end, Zeus 5 — the newest American manned moon probe, currently in orbit around the moon, will suffer a dramatic and unfortunate accident during re-entry.'

Donahue stood up. 'You can't,' he shouted. 'You can't.'

Professor Petrov smiled. 'But yes, Mr Donahue — of course.'

Feeling a little sick Donahue sat down on the chair again. His hands began to sweat. Although the launch of Zeus 5 had been widely covered by press reports and by TV and radio, he had been unable to pay full attention to it because of pre-occupation with his assignment. Now Y181 was to be used to murder three brave men — American astronauts on their way back home to earth. The idea appalled him.

Petrov spoke again. 'Any re-entering capsule makes an ideal infrared source for a homing missile and of course radio communication with ground control is not possible because of the plasma sheath. The world will simply believe that something went terribly wrong during the re-entry phase.

'That is my project, Mr Donahue.'

Simon Donahue was horrified. His brain refused to accept that it was going to happen. He opened his mouth to speak and closed it again without saying anything.

'Do you not think it a splendid plan, Englishman?' Professor Petrov stared at Donahue. 'Using a British device to destroy an American capsule.'

Donahue felt helpless. It was bound to succeed, it was all so very simple and so very obvious. He could do nothing and nobody else could be expected to do anything; no one would even begin to suspect the reason for the tragic burning up of Zeus 5. Donahue could imagine the screaming horror of the moment for the three astronauts although he supposed they would never know what had happened. A sudden flare on the radar at Houston would be all that earth would ever see of the returning capsule. Five hundred thousand miles to be incinerated in a fraction of a second. The idea was awful.

He stood up. 'The great Soviet Republic is a pack of bastards.' he said slowly. 'If this is the way you intend to lead the world in scientific prowess — God help humanity! I hope the bloody submarine blows up when you launch the rocket. I hope the whole damned lot of you go with it.'

Petrov spoke to the small man, then to Donahue.

'Please sit down Donahue; you can do nothing.'

Donahue continued to stand.

'Sit down!' Petrov was much bigger than Donahue and now stood facing him.

Donahue slumped back onto the chair. 'Why have you told me all this?' he said.

The smaller Russian — if he was a Russian, which Donahue doubted, said. 'Why not?'

'As you are going to the Soviet Union as an enemy agent where you will be thoroughly questioned and subsequently imprisoned or shot, it seemed to us that you might be interested in learning the consequences of your failure.'

The perverse logic of this had not been lost on Donahue. That his mission had been unsuccessful and was probably going to cost him his life was bad enough. There was no need to remind him that his incompetence would, in a few days time, cause the fiery death of three other men high above the earth's surface. The loss of prestige to the west was of no consequence compared with the deliberate cold-blooded murder that these men were planning.

'I should like to return to my cabin,' he said.

'Certainly.' Petrov pushed a button on the grey steel desk at his side. 'There are bigger things to play with than bows and arrows, Mr Donahue.'

Donahue duly followed the officer back to his cabin and sank onto his stretcher staring unblinkingly as the door clanged shut.

8

For the remainder of the day Donahue thought furiously. Once over the initial shock he was able to come quickly to terms with the idea that on board this ship was a team of men whose primary purpose it was to assist in a scheme to destroy Zeus 5.

It was a simple matter for him to resolve to prevent this terrible plan from being undertaken. If he was to lose his life in the attempt — he would at least have tried.

Donahue had never believed that he was a brave man. Often, he had wondered if there were men who could face real danger without a sense of fear. If there were, then he was not to be counted amongst their number. At Cape Alvera he remembered thinking that to destroy Y181 when he had the chance would almost certainly have caused his death. Bitterly he realized now that he should have done it. Locked in his steel cell he was completely powerless.

There were two possibilities — the porthole and the brief time when the cabin door was open to admit the seaman who brought food. If his leg had been uninjured his chances would perhaps be a little better — but only a little he thought. All his pockets were empty. He had no equipment, four days in which to act and his own wits.

Donahue realized that in fact he did not have four days; he didn't know how long it would be before the rendezvous with the submarine. To ready the missile for launch from the sub would, he estimated, take at least a day — probably more. Once the device left the *Vertaz* there would be no chance of interfering with the Soviet plan.

Wild and improbable schemes raced through Simon Donahue's mind. Break into the Radio room and make contact with the base at Hawaii — contaminate the ships water supply: all were improbable in conception to say nothing of the practical difficulties of carrying them out.

Donahue forced his brain to throw up an endless succession of possible plans.

After several hours he had got nowhere and was mentally exhausted. He began to make a systematic detailed inspection of the cabin.

The porthole was about twenty feet above the sea as far as he could judge, although the estimate was necessarily crude because Donahue could not look straight downwards. Steel clamps, holding the glass against the seal were tightly frozen in their brackets from corrosion. He tried banging one with a pole taken from his stretcher but to no avail. The effort made his leg begin to hurt. Donahue was not at all sure that he could have climbed through the tiny hole in the hull even if he could have managed to open the port. What he would have done once outside was quite unknown anyway.

Almost certainly, the cabin door was the only answer.

The engines of the spy ship had not altered frequency since they had first begun to rumble when Donahue had been brought on board. As far as he could tell they had not altered course during the voyage either, although he could not be absolutely sure of that. The Pacific is a large place and Donahue realized that he had not the slightest idea where the rendezvous was going to be made. Consequently, he would be quite unable to radio his position even if he managed by some means or other to secure the ship's transmitter.

If anything was to be done it would have to be done by Simon Donahue alone. Totally and utterly alone. One man pitted against a whole Soviet spy ship. The odds were very, very long.

The inside of the cabin door had no handle. He guessed he was imprisoned in a storage locker of some kind. Heavy steel hinges were welded to the door and there was no trace of a gap between it and the frame. Donahue pushed it tentatively but did not bother to exert any real force. It was pointless trying.

By lunch time Donahue had given up thinking of any plan of escape but one. There was only one.

The first part was easily formulated — for the rest he would have to rely on improvisation.

As soon as the inevitable unappetizing bowl of soup was brought to his cabin he began to become more active. There was no point delaying his move until tomorrow — to-night was his best chance.

When the sailor returned for the tray, Donahue watched his every movement with intense concentration. Perhaps if the man had been more perceptive he might have sensed the fact that he was being studied by the lean Englishman casually lying on his bunk.

Donahue had until evening to gather his thoughts, get some rest and try to control his fear.

Certain minor preparations could be undertaken before the sailor reappeared with Donahue's dinner.

Firstly he removed the wooden poles from each side of his stretcher, then, placing one across the other on the floor, Donahue stood on the cross. There was a splintering crack and he had eighteen inches of solid timber to serve as a crude weapon.

The stretcher was easily reassembled by pushing the broken ends of the pole firmly together inside the canvas tube. It would just support itself propped on the two boxes but Donahue dare no longer sit on it. Instead, he sat on one of the wooden crates whilst he carefully rebandaged his leg which was now less painful although still extremely stiff. The wound had not yet closed properly and Donahue thought that any severe exertion would probably start the bleeding again. He would have to be careful with it.

Next he removed both leather laces from his hunting boots and laboriously chewed one in half. Each half was sufficiently long to relace each boot using only the top few eyelets of each. He tied two-inch loops in the ends of the spare lace and tested the strength of it by subjecting it to a series of violent tugs. He put the lace in the pocket of his jeans.

It was unfortunate that he had been unable to shave since the beginning of his imprisonment. However, he was blessed with a very slow growing beard and although his face felt uncomfortable from the stubble he doubted if it would be noticed at a casual glance.

There was nothing else to do now but to wait patiently for evening.

He lay on the warm steel floor, head upon rolled up blanket and tried to sleep.

Donahue dozed fitfully for part of the afternoon but as the sunlight through the porthole slowly faded he became progressively more and more awake. Finally, when it was dusk, the tiny bulb in the ceiling began to light the cabin with a dull yellow glow.

Donahue rose to his knees and vomited twice uncontrollably into his slops bucket. He had been unable to empty the bucket because of the seized porthole and had got used to the smell of his own waste. The sick smelt vile. He felt cold and nervous. There was less than half an hour to wait now.

When the sailor opened the door the English prisoner was sitting on the

135

wooden crate at the end of his bed, legs crossed. Donahue nodded at him taking the tray.

Alone again, Simon Donahue knew that this was where it started.

It was fortunate that the American Astronauts could have no idea of the drama about to be enacted back on earth.

Donahue forced himself to eat the daily apple, disposing the remainder of the meal in his bucket. Then, sliding one box towards the centre of the bed to support the longest section of the broken pole he withdrew his primitive weapon.

Heart beating furiously and stomach churning the minutes passed.

When he returned, the Russian was not surprised to see Donahue standing up leaning with both palms against the wall peering through the dark porthole into the night. Since he had arrived on board, the Englishman had appeared subdued. It had been explained that he was a British spy being taken back home to Russia. The sailor thought things would be pretty tough for the Englishman when the *Vertaz* arrived home.

He bent down to collect the tray. Much too late he sensed the rapid movement.

Donahue wheeled round withdrawing the length of wood held flat against his belly by his belt. With one savage downwards movement the club smashed sickeningly onto the back of the sailors head. He pitched forward onto the tray and lay quite still.

Donahue moved quickly. Experience had taught him that you could work much faster if you tried not to hurry but his control was inadequate and his hands were trembling again.

With some difficulty he dragged the limp body over to the stretcher and propped it up. He thought the man looked dead.

Exploring the back of the sailor's head with his fingers Donahue felt a deep crack in the skull.

There was not time to find out whether he was dead or not. Anyway it didn't matter.

Donahue hated killing but on this occasion it somehow seemed totally unimportant to him.

The Russian's sweater of coarse blue wool was a snug fit. He regretted substituting it for his leather jerkin but even a simple disguise could easily gain those extra vital seconds in a chance encounter. Boots and jeans he retained, these being close enough to conventional wear on board the *Vertaz* to pass unnoticed.

Slipping the length of stretcher pole into the waist of his jeans and picking up the dinner knife from the floor he pushed open the door very gently.

The corridor looked as it had looked earlier in the day when he had been taken to see Petrov. At regular intervals the lights left gloomy yellow patches on the walls and floor.

Outside the cabin the engine noise was much louder. Donahue waited for his ears to become accustomed to the throb before moving away.

He knew that the only exit from the corridor was the ladder at the far end — unless one of the numerous closed doors concealed some other passageway.

138

Donahue wanted to go down, not up, but there seemed no choice.

Purposefully he moved from the protective shelter of the doorway shutting the door of the cabin behind him.

How long it would be before the sailor was missed Donahue didn't know. The first place they would look would be the cabin — and then the hunt would be on.

He limped down the corridor and climbed the short ladder to the landing above. This time he could see that he was at the centre of a cross, a junction of four passages leading away from him, each at ninety degrees to the other. Donahue had no idea which one to take. Two of them would run fore and aft, the others necessarily would be shorter.

From the gentle rolling of the *Vertaz* as she sailed on through the summer night, Donahue believed that he was amidships. This belief was reinforced by the distinct feeling that his cabin had been towards the stern.

He chose the passageway directly ahead of him.

The sound of an opening door on the deck below near the ladder echoed up the companionway as he began to move.

There were two or maybe three choices. Fight, hide or hope that the person or persons would pass him by unrecognized.

Footsteps stopped at the base of the ladder.

He ran forward to the cabin where he had been taken earlier in the day, pushed on the door handle and burst in, wooden club drawn ready.

Chuck, the big man from the Cape, stared stupidly at Donahue crouching in the entrance. Donahue leant on the door with his back, watching the other man intently.

The big man looked very frightened.

'Very gently, Chuck,' Donahue spoke quietly.

Chuck was perhaps fifty pounds heavier than Donahue and had two good legs. To the Russian however, the Englishman looked very menacing. He had drawn the knife which he held in his left hand and his eyes were dangerous.

The Russian remained standing in the

centre of the floor a thin book held loosely in his hand.

Donahue wondered if he was as harmless as he looked. Then he remembered David Marshall. This man with his little smiling companion had murdered David. Donahue thought he would be well advised to be cautious.

Chuck slowly put the book on the table, his eyes never leaving Donahue.

It was too obvious.

The length of wood smashed down on the Russian's fingers long before they reached the button.

Donahue heard and felt the bones crack.

The tip of the little finger was smashed to a pulp, its end fanned out like a chewed matchstick.

Holding his hand to his stomach the big man reeled against the wall.

Donahue was taking no chances now.

He walked towards the Russian and thrust the jagged end of the wood against the injured hand with all his weight.

The man gasped and slid backwards down the wall.

Deep holes in the shattered hand left by the splintered end of the stretcher pole began to fill with blood as the Russian tried desperately to take a breath. Donahue's thrust had badly winded him.

Just as Donahue thought Chuck wasn't going to make it, the collapsed lungs managed to open allowing the Russian to noisily suck in gulps of air.

He rolled onto his side retching horribly still nursing his bloody hand.

Donahue felt sick again and was trembling violently.

'Chuck, listen to me,' he said.

'You have to take me to the engine room — now!'

The man was in too much pain to understand. His eyes were glazed as he looked at Donahue.

'The engine room — where is it?' Donahue raised his club.

God he hated this. There must be a better way.

Like a sorrowful dog, slowly the Russian shook his head. Several small red pools were forming on the deck plates from the dripping hand.

'You will, Chuck, or I'll break your other hand,' Donahue put as much menace in his voice as he could muster.

'Come on.'

He gripped the front of the Russian's shirt and slid him back up the wall until the man was on his feet.

'I'll follow you.' Donahue wrenched open the door standing aside as the big man tottered through. If there had been anyone in the corridor Donahue would have had no chance. He was in a hurry now — it could only be minutes before the sailor in the cabin was discovered.

Bent double with pain, his shattered hand held against him, Chuck moved ahead down the passageway. Behind, club gripped firmly, limped Simon Donahue.

After what seemed to be an eternity the end was reached, where another steel ladder inevitably disappeared into the gloom.

Donahue waved the Russian down.

With great difficulty he started the descent, Donahue keeping several feet above and watching warily for any hostile move. Whilst unlikely — it could be possible for Chuck to reach up with his good hand and grab Donahue's injured leg.

In fact the trip was uneventful apart from Donahue's foot almost slipping off one rung of the ladder thickly smeared with blood from Chuck's hand.

The *Vertaz* was quite unlike any ship Donahue had ever been on. Long dreary corridors with those extraordinary shafts at the end, the incredible number of steel doors — all seemingly identical, Donahue wondered how the crew found their way around.

Throughout the descent, the engine noise became steadily greater until soon it became quite painful to the ears. He could smell hot oil in the air around him. The atmosphere in the shaft was stifling.

At the bottom Donahue waved the Russian away from the ladder. The hammering throb of the engines pounded painfully through Donahue's head.

An enormous door swung gently on hinges ahead of them. A sign, printed in Russian was bolted crookedly to it.

Donahue left Chuck at the foot of the ladder and approached what he believed to be the engine room. Between door and frame he could see catwalks of expanded metal mesh and the heads of the huge eight cylinder Russian marine diesel.

He stepped back pulling Chuck to the opening. There was no-one to be seen from their vantage point. Donahue dragged Chuck through the door hurrying to a particularly dark area of the room in the shadow of a tall air duct. He pointed suddenly back towards the door. Chuck turned. For the second time that evening, the short wooden club thudded onto an unprotected skull.

The Russian sank first to his knees then over onto his side. He lay awkwardly, legs spread grotesquely across a shallow pool of steaming water.

Donahue regretted the brutality. He had been treated well since being captured and it was difficult to justify the type of punishment he was dealing out. Quite how much brutality Marshall had been subjected to in Oregon Donahue didn't know. That he had finally been killed by Chuck or the small man gave Donahue some small comfort when thinking analytically of his present behaviour.

It was hard to believe that the engine room was totally deserted. Perhaps he had already been detected. There was no way of knowing.

Cautiously he looked around the corner of the air duct.

Donahue realized with sinking heart that now he had completed the first part of his plan, he had no idea how to stop the *Vertaz*.

Time was running out.

9

Almost exactly seven thousand miles due east from the *Vertaz* Jane Marshall stared out of her bedroom window and wondered.

In London, Francis Goddard had not yet found time to go home from his office. Papers littered his normally tidy desk. He was more than usually tired.

Both Jane and Goddard had thought of Simon Donahue a great deal that day.

Jane had experienced the familiar empty feeling before. Never had she been able to persuade Simon to discuss his work and she frequently wondered what the trips abroad were for. Why sometimes when he returned his hands shook and his eyes were empty. Where was he now? What was he doing?

Goddard had sixteen projects to worry about. Three of them were bound to be unsuccessful. Included in this category was Y181. No communication of any kind had been received from Donahue since the receipt of an uncoded cable announcing his intention to do some hunting at Cape Alvera. It was impossible to say where Donahue was now, consequently Goddard had really stopped speculating several days ago.

The Y181 file remained a slim volume. He could almost visualize the red outline of the 'Closed/Incomplete' stamp on the cover.

There were other men who were not thinking of Simon Donahue. They had other urgent matters to occupy them.

Three of them were a quarter of a million miles away from the planet that was their home. Watching and monitoring every move they made were countless hundreds of trained engineers and scientists scattered over the United States and other countries of the Western World.

To all of these people, the actions of one man — an escaped prisoner on board a Russian spy ship — were to be of the utmost importance over the next few hours.

★ ★ ★

Fortunately, Donahue had not had the time to consider in detail the wider implications of his bid to stop the launch of the Soviet missile. To prevent the destruction of Zeus 5 and to keep alive were simple enough immediate aims.

Jane had drifted into his mind at various times, especially when he had been camped in the rain forest. On several assignments he had used her as a reason for going on, for making that last impossible effort to bring him through. Since his stay at the Cape her image had begun to fade. Annoyingly he was not able to recall her as vividly as he wished.

Now in the pulsating heart of the *Vertaz* he tried to establish a firm reason for continuing with this hopeless task.

Against the enormous engines he was powerless. Soon, in this dark, hot, noisy room, he would be found alone. They would know why he was there — they would be pleased to have found him in time.

Donahue mentally shook himself. A ridiculous expression was repeating itself continually in his head. 'Gird up your loins, gird up your loins,' over and over it went.

He grinned inwardly wondering where his brain had dragged such an unoriginal quotation from.

Engine noise is a difficult thing to become accustomed to. It was difficult to think properly but think he must.

A final sweeping glance showed that the dim compartment was still apparently unoccupied although it was impossible for him to be absolutely sure because of the poor illumination.

Stepping from the protective shadow of the ducting Donahue began to reconnoitre, walking along the catwalk looking downwards into the roaring pit.

There were other levels — one above him, one below. Maintenance bays lined one end of the lower walkway, perhaps there would be tools he could use in one of them.

Swiftly, calf aching, Donahue climbed down yet another ladder cursing the designer of the Russian ship.

The second bay contained a sturdy work bench of oil-stained wood and, to Donahue's surprise, standing in a corner a portable oxyacetylene welding kit mounted on a wheeled trolley.

Here at last was something that could be used to inflict an enormous amount of damage if expertly used, and Simon Donahue knew how to use it.

It was pointless to explore further. A torch like this was as good a sabotage device as he could have hoped to find.

Would there be time to use it?

If only the wretched gas hoses would reach the catwalk above he could weld the door shut giving himself some extra time in which to work. There may be other ways into the room though — he hadn't time to check on that.

Pulling the trolley over the corrugated surface of the metal mesh proved more difficult than he had anticipated. Frequently the small wheels became firmly stuck causing Donahue to exert more load on his leg than was desirable. However, after several minutes he had managed to manoeuvre the unit close enough to a group of three pipes clamped together against the side of the engine crankcase.

He reached for matches remembering with a shock that they were still in his jerkin.

Donahue ran back to the bay hoping to find a flint lighter commonly used with oxyacetylene outfits.

There it was, lying on the bench. Perhaps his luck was changing — or at least holding.

By the time he had lit the gas and roughly adjusted the flame he was soaked in perspiration from exertion, nerves and the intense heat.

Opening the valves on the torch handle to obtain the fiercest heat that could be used safely without the danger of it self-extinguishing, Donahue approached the group of feed pipes. He had no idea what they contained. The fact that they ran adjacent to the engine was encouraging but there was no quick way of assessing their importance to the vital functioning of the big diesel.

He applied the cone of the blue flame to the underside of the lowest steel pipe. His plan was to work upwards, taking each individually.

Luck had not deserted Simon Donahue.

Oil at one hundred degrees centigrade driven by a pressure of eighty five pounds per square inch spurted from the small pin hole burnt by the torch.

It smelt like lubricating oil.

Slowly he moved the flame upwards around the circumference of the tube until the pinhole became a slot and the slot became a larger slot.

Precious life blood of the engine gushed violently from the severed artery. A fan of dark brown liquid over four inches wide and now nearly a half an inch across squirted smoothly under Donahue's hand disappearing through the grating on which he stood.

The man with the cutting flame had no mercy although heat from the oil made it increasingly uncomfortable to hold the torch. More and more of the steel from the wall was progressively melted away until the roar of escaping oil was as loud as the engine.

He was smothered in oil and hardly able to breathe through the clouds of acrid smoke produced by the action of the liquid passing over the white hot edges of jagged hole.

When the aperture was as large as the bore of the pipe he stepped back taking welcome breaths of relatively pure air leaving the torch, still alight, wedged between the top two pipes.

Eyes that have been watching acetylene gas burning in pure oxygen are not able to perform in conditions of near darkness for some time afterwards. Donahue could no longer see across the dim room to the door.

He wondered how long it would take for the oil loss to become effective. Automatic warning indicators would cut the fuel supply before bearing failure — providing they were fitted. If they weren't, it would be a good idea to vacate the engine compartment as quickly as possible.

He did not believe that the diesel could continue to run to destruction — surely oil pressure would be monitored some-where.

Climbing with oil-soaked boots was hazardous but he was back in the shelter of the air duct beside the still unconscious Chuck in only a few moments.

Still the diesel ran.

Donahue did not know that all engine feed lines were monitored and displayed on a complex control panel over fifty feet from the diesel in a soundproofed room. He didn't know that the Chief Engineer was at dinner in the mess and that his assistant — a dull ignorant seaman from Urkutsk — was not following the simple written instructions by watching the three essential gauges in the control room. It was not possible for the unfortunate man to serve this vital watch. Comrade Seranavitch lay quite dead in the cabin of the English prisoner.

Simon Donahue changed his oil-soaked sweater with the much larger one worn by Chuck. As an afterthought he searched the pockets of the limp body discovering nothing of use except some matches.

Thoughtfully opening the box he struck one, holding the flame underneath the slippery crumpled ball of oily wool. The sweater smouldered and then began to burn.

Swiftly, ignoring the dull pain in his leg, he ran round the catwalk until he was above the oil leak.

The blazing ball dropped between the engine and the edge of the catwalk below leaving a trail of blue swirling smoke hanging in the air.

Whether or not it would ignite the gallons of oil that must now be swilling about underneath the engine he didn't know. Donahue had done what he could. Now it was time to think of himself.

The labyrinth of corridors must be faced — somehow or other he would have to find his way to the upper deck of the *Vertaz*.

Without incident he reached the top of the companionway. The rungs of the ladder continued upwards through the ceiling of the corridor along which Chuck had brought him.

Revived by the cooler air Donahue

continued his ascent. A further passage-way was passed before he found himself in surroundings more similar to those encountered in ocean going freighters.

By this time it was obvious that the crew of the *Vertaz* must be extremely small and he guessed that they would consist largely of specialists to service and control the complex equipment carried by the spy ship. This would explain why fortunately he had not encountered crew members in his recent wanderings.

He had not properly closed the door of the engine room. Behind him now the smell of burning oil was noticeable, rising up the shaft.

Ahead, and to the left, or to port, Donahue supposed he should call it, a short flight of steps led to fresh air. He could smell the clean saltness of it.

Unchallenged he reached the top deck. It was the first fresh air he had breathed for four days. Now he must consider escape.

Above, the sky gleamed with a million stars twinkling down on a placid smooth Pacific. Mortally wounded with night lights set the *Vertaz* left a creamy green black wake writhing behind her as she sailed on to meet her silent companion from beneath the oceans' surface.

★ ★ ★

Conditions in the engine room had changed drastically since the saboteur had left. Lodged between the pipes, the burning welding torch had continued its evil work. Now all lines under the clamp were severed. The upper two were main fuel supply feeds. Many gallons of diesel oil now lay mixed with lubricating oil to a depth of nearly six inches in the pit around the engine.

Long before starved bearings started to grip the steel journals of the whirling crankshaft in a prelude to seizure, the atmosphere outside the engine was thick with wreathing fumes from local pockets of burning oil.

The spine of the *Vertaz* began to shudder as the mighty diesel ground to a tortured shrieking halt.

There was no spectacular explosion, no

violent internal rupture of over-stressed metal — just a series of enormous vibrations transmitted through the whole hull followed by an uncanny silence.

Alarms rang.

On deck, Simon Donahue knew he had succeeded in stopping the *Vertaz*. He moved cautiously to the cover of a large hatchway crouching close to the cool steel rectangle.

Below, the strange long corridors choked with smoke making it impossible for the crew to man their fire posts.

Five men wearing breathing apparatus eventually reached the entrance to the engine room using powerful flashlights to guide them. Smoke poured through the gap left by the half open door billowing as though it was a powdered solid.

Fighting searing radiated heat they opened the door as wide as possible securing it to the bulkhead.

It was a bad mistake.

Although the shaft containing the ladder was acting efficiently as a chimney for the mixture of oils burning hotly in the engine room, in reverse it could also admit new air rich in oxygen.

For a moment it seemed that the smoke flowed backwards through the entrance before the billowing resumed. There were two such pauses — after each, the burning appeared more violent.

On the third gulp, sufficient air was drawn back down the shaft to provide a perfectly combustible mixture.

The explosion was tremendous.

Like a puppet ship in a television studio the *Vertaz* heaved as her starboard plates burst asunder.

A hideous red mushroom of hot gas shot from the rent in her double-skins of steel plate.

Five men along with the big Russian Chuck were flattened like plasticine dolls by the pressure before being instantly cremated. Other men in the lower areas of the ship suffered haemorrhage from shock waves and lay screaming, blood pouring from ears, noses and mouths.

In the Radar Control Centre two others were killed instantaneously by the direct short of the magnetron power supply to earth. Fifteen thousand volts in a micro-second pulse ended their lives quickly and painlessly.

No one had any idea of what had happened. Some of the older hands believed from hard-earned experience gained long ago in the North Sea that the *Vertaz* had been torpedoed.

There was panic.

Men fought their way through smoke-filled passageways only to collapse coughing horribly before reaching the open.

The *Vertaz* had watertight compartments as well as a good double-skinned hull. If the party sent to the engine room had closed the door instead of opening it, there might have been perhaps a chance for the stricken vessel.

Burning oil spread rapidly over the surface of the sea illuminating the *Vertaz* in a nightmare glare of crimson. Gallon upon gallon poured from the dreadful wound displaced by water rushing to take its place.

Soon it was much quieter along the corridors. Sea water crested with oily slime crept coldly into the veins of the

Russian ship, seeking out every nook and cranny.

Men trapped in cabins — doors stuck fast by distortion of deck plates and bulkheads — saw with horror the first trickles running over their feet.

Things were a little better for those who had been working in the upper levels.

Despite the angle at which the *Vertaz* was lying now, she was still relatively stable, the tons of water acting as sluggish ballast. Luckily her emergency radio was still operational allowing a stream of messages to be relayed from the powerful transmitter.

The captain — an efficient man who had commanded three other spy ships before the *Vertaz*, had very precise instructions regarding procedures to be followed under circumstances such as these. Coded signals flashed around the Communist world for over sixteen minutes before any indication of the plight of the *Vertaz* was broadcast.

At last, whilst the 'Mayday' signal went out, the captain and first officer attended to the destruction of certain vital documents including microfilm copies of the Astra Physics drawings. The act was of little consequence to them, duplicates, they knew were already safe in Moscow which would allow further models of Y181 to be produced again one day.

Shortly after the alarm had sounded, Petrov had approached the captain but there was no question of saving the sunseeker unless the submarine could guarantee to reach the *Vertaz* before any other potential rescue vessel.

Y181 was carefully sealed in a special weighted container. As soon as a pressure of five atmospheres was reached on the journey to the ocean bed a pressure transducer would trigger an internal acid capsule. Before the order to abandon ship was announced over the public address speakers, Y181 in its metal coffin lay at rest on the sandy bed of the Pacific. If by some remote chance it were to be recovered within a period of two hours perhaps it would be recognizable, thereafter there would be nothing whatever to identify.

That the Soviet ship would ultimately sink there was no doubt. Designed into the hull were destruct mechanisms to ensure that the spy ship either would live normally or quickly die; there were no permissible intermediate states.

On the bridge four red lights flashed on simultaneously.

In exactly twenty-six minutes, if the *Vertaz* had not sunk beneath the surface, seventy explosive bolts would blast open another hole — this one carefully located for maximum internal flooding.

Cursing fluently, stumbling in the eerie red light from the burning fuel, stretcher parties assembled the wounded on deck to shouted instructions. More of the crew had survived than the captain had originally believed. Seventeen were wounded and twenty-four men with three officers were either dead or unaccounted for. Under the superstructure supporting the now stationary radar reflector the remainder stood silently in a frightened group.

There was an obvious problem.

A thousand times before, a naval

captain had been presented with the same stupid problem. It is not difficult to evolve a design allowing life boats to be launched when the ship is at a dangerous angle but the *Vertaz*, like innumerable others, had not been made with this facility in mind. Cleverness and sophistication used in the design of her electronic systems had not been extended to the simple consideration of life preservation.

Boats could easily be lowered over the starboard side now that the *Vertaz* was listing badly in that quarter. The davits could not however lower the port boats without the danger of them crashing into the sloping side of the hull. To starboard, for the entire length of the vessel and extending away nearly one hundred feet from the hull raged an inferno of blazing oil.

The captain made the only choice, ordering the wounded to be placed in two of the port boats. These were lowered as slowly as possible until keels touched the plates of the *Vertaz*, then, at a critically dangerous angle allowed to slide down the hull to the water until finally they bobbed in the shadow of their crippled parent ship.

Under the command of the officers, one after another, men climbed over the rails and slid down the wet side of the *Vertaz* hitting the sea at impossible angles, arms and legs flailing.

All reached the boats, including the captain — most unharmed except for bruises but two with broken arms where foolishly they had hit the side of one of the craft below.

Keeping in the shadow of the Russian ship the little boats moved away from the oil fire. From a quarter of a mile away they watched a tragic unforgettable scene as the *Vertaz* disappeared silently and gracefully into the writhing pool of flames.

Occasionally there was a dull bump as their life boats collided with floating wreckage driven earlier from the ship by the explosion. Hatches and other unidentifiable flotsam bobbed all around them in the dark.

Rescue lights were set, a line passed from one boat to the other and the wait began, each man thinking that he was lucky not to be still on board the *Vertaz*.

There are many worse places to be adrift than the Pacific Ocean on a still summer night. Help would already be on its way — there was little concern in the life boats.

10

When young Bobby Antigo had taken his training course for Air Crew Mechanic it had been said unkindly that he did not know, and would never know, whether he was punched or bored. In transferring to Radio Operator, Class 5B, he had hoped to discover that any natural aptitude that he had was more closely aligned with electronics. When this proved beyond all doubt not to be the case, wisely he had concluded that the unfortunate Mr and Mrs Antigo were to blame by either in some way neglecting his education or because he had inherited some of their inherent traits of stupidity. Bobby had always thought that he deserved better parents.

The United States Air Force did not regard Bobby as a failure however. To do that would be to group over half of their men under the same heading. Rather, Private Antigo was thought to be good basic material but as yet not adequately trained. It was an attitude precisely similar to that of any animal trainer.

To-night, Bobby had reported to Building Six for radio duty at ten hundred hours, relieving Bill Steinberg who, as usual, had been draped comfortably over the equipment table. Bobby envied operators who could go to sleep on duty, it demonstrated that you were on top of your job and had no worries. The best he had ever been able to do was to artificially relax with his feet up, occasionally awkwardly chewing gum at the same time as smoking a cigarette.

Conveniently located on the north coast of the Midway Islands of the Hawaiian Group, the USAF radio headquarters received every transmission for a radius of nearly six thousand miles. The vast majority of these had nothing whatever to do with the United States Air Force which made listening a fascinating past-time for bored personnel.

During his watch, as a member of Air Sea Rescue, Bobby Antigo had only to listen for distress calls which, as he had been repeatedly told, would one day be bound to happen during his alert period.

No one had ever picked up a distress signal in Shack Six since Bobby had been stationed on the island. If one was to occur he knew beyond question that it would not be whilst he was in charge; long experience had shown that nothing ever happened to Bobby.

When after a dreary hour's listening the 'Mayday' call crackled out from the speaker in the receiver console, Bobby had nearly fallen backwards out of the big swivel chair. Mouth open, unable and unwilling to believe that he had suddenly been chosen for such greatness, he had listened to the repeated signal giving the position of the *Vertaz*.

The weeks of training, the pages of untidy notes and the two volumes of 'Procedures/ASR/USAF' had been immediately and absolutely forgotten. Like a frightened rabbit Bobby had run to Rescue Headquarters some one hundred and twenty yards down the concrete strip which connected all buildings of Air Sea Rescue.

The patient lieutenant had taken at least a minute calming him down and in trying to obtain a moderately coherent statement of the trouble.

Calmly they had returned to the shack where luckily the signals were still being received.

Never since its inception had ASR been lucky enough to be called by a Russian Survey ship, let alone one apparently on fire nearly eighteen hundred miles away. Now they could demonstrate their incredible efficiency — now they could show those lousy marines in the West Sector that the United States Pacific Rescue Team was a real organization.

From then on it had been a case of one misfortune after another. To crown the whole sorry affair there were no aircraft — two were in bits and three others had been taken out somewhere, nobody knew where. The two in the hanger were always in pieces, these were the aircraft that the mechanics played with. It was said that there used to be three but that now only enough parts were left to assemble two.

A Canadian CL28 of the submarine hunter class had been visiting the air strip and it was this rather elderly aircraft that finally had been despatched to seek the *Vertaz*.

It took six hours to locate the two tiny life boats.

The Canadian CL28 was a good plane for flying slowly; to find submarines it is essential to have excellent low speed characteristics. It was this that made the old aircraft especially suitable for this type of work although the American Air Sea Rescue, until now, had never even considered it.

At four hours forty eight, fierce white searchlights housed in plexiglass domes on the leading edge of each wing picked out all that was left of the *Vertaz*.

Long before the plane had reached the scene, where now it circled in the dark radioing the precise position of the survivors and advising Hawaii of weather conditions, the nearest vessel had been located and told of her duty.

Ironically, the *Fraser*, out of Vancouver, a small freighter used to ship anything that would pay the insurance and keep the owner/captain in whisky for the voyage, was by maritime standards extremely close to the Russians. Although Hawaii could not be entirely sure owing to the somewhat curt message received, it seemed that the *Fraser* could make contact in only two hours. She had seen the smoke and flames in the night and was already steaming towards the last radioed position of the distressed Soviet ship.

In fact, it was more than four hours before what remained of the Russian crew saw the grimy Canadian freighter through the dawn light. The CL28 had left only half an hour before.

By the time that all men were safely on board the *Fraser* and Canadian and Russian captains had exchanged pleasantries, the sun was well clear of the horizon.

During the night, despite numerous plausible theories, no one in the life boats had been able to say definitely what had happened on the *Vertaz* although several guesses had come close to the truth.

It was possible that the English prisoner had escaped, subsequently sabotaging the ship killing himself in the process but nobody would ever know exactly what had caused the explosion.

Once on board the *Fraser*, with much gestulating and interruption from Professor Petrov and other Russians who could speak English, the bewildered captain of the Canadian ship finally managed to gather a rather imprecise picture of what had happened.

He was bound for Hawaii carrying a shipment of canned fruit. This had been produced originally in Hawaii then shipped to Canada to be subsequently re-exported back to Hawaii. The captain had long ceased to marvel at the intricacies of international trade; it was a valuable cargo and he enjoyed the Islands — why speculate on the foolishness of the respective governments.

The detour to rescue these damned Reds was a nuisance. He hoped, rather in vain he thought looking at them, that they wouldn't drink.

Wreckage still floated on the calm sea, much of it spread around the *Fraser* as she began to move away to clear water.

No sooner had her props begun to churn than a shout echoed from the bows.

'Stop engines — quick for God's sake — Sir.'

Several men ran to the rail where one of the *Fraser*'s crew was pointing down.

Forty feet to port, tied to a short length of wood, a man's head bobbed in the slight swell caused by the transient movement of the ship.

One of the Canadians, apparently especially partial to water — he had spent most of the time during the rescue of the Russians swimming aimlessly around the life boats — dived from the deck entering the sea neatly with hardly a splash.

Soon, streaked in rust from the hull, the sodden body was hauled limply over the side by a canvas sling attached to the end of a stout rope, the aquatic Canadian following afterwards a huge grin on his face.

'I think he's alive,' he said.

'Look at his throat.'

Beneath the man's chin, against his windpipe, was a wooden beam, a rough length of pine about four inches square and three feet long. Passing round the back of the neck, holding the massively heavy spar to the body, was a leather thong.

Lifting the body from the water had caused the leather to bite even more deeply into the flesh of the neck until it was completely embedded in a deep red weal.

Willing hands supported the wood whilst the leather was cut and pulled gently from the bloody groove.

Simon Donahue, nine tenths dead, was carried below for badly needed medical attention.

Powerless, the Russians watched.

Donahue had been caught totally unawares when the explosion had occurred. In the dark, squatting against the hatch aperture he had been thrown with great violence against something very solid before the long fall to the cold water had brought him suddenly to his senses.

In seconds the fuel oil fire seeping from the ruptured hull had caused him to swim frantically along the side of the still moving ship until the stern slipped past. Then, thankful that the props were motionless, with long powerful strokes he had swum away from the ship and fire until his arms refused to function any longer.

He had certainly stopped the *Vertaz*, Zeus 5 would be safe but what of himself?

Not daring to swim or splash in case of attracting attention, Donahue had watched the life boats being lowered, grimly illuminated by flickering red light.

If he were alive the Russians would not run the risk of the English prisoner reporting the true mission of the *Vertaz*. If they found him defenceless in the water he was as good as dead.

Donahue had no doubt that rescue would take place within a matter of hours. Until then he must be silent.

So, for those long, long cold numb hours, less than a quarter of a mile from the two life boats, Donahue had kept very still in the dark.

Bumping into the wooden spar had been a stroke of good fortune. For half the night he had lain motionless on top of it until he knew that in another quarter of an hour or so he would have to let go forever.

In his pocket the leather thong he had made for a strangle loop was turned into a garotte for his own head. Several abortive attempts to tie himself to the spar showed that, if he was to become unconscious, the only safe way was to fasten the wood securely under his chin ensuring that his face would always float clear of the water. It hurt if he stopped taking the strain with his arms but by the time they could no longer support him he was insensitive to pain.

Whilst the CL28 circled noisily over-head floodlighting the sea, Donahue offered one final prayer that he wouldn't be seen until help arrived before slipping gratefully into unconsciousness, the wet thong biting harshly into the flesh of his neck.

Circumstances had favoured Donahue since the beginning of his plan to save Zeus 5. The weather had been kind, he had spent the time in the water hidden by darkness and the *Fraser* had arrived at exactly the right time, dawn.

Looking back over the whole business as he lay in a comfortable bunk below in the freighter he thought that he didn't deserve the kind of luck that fate had seen fit to deal him on that night.

There was no doctor on board, instead, the first mate administered primitive medicine to Donahue using a well thumbed text book as a guide to good practice.

An enormous bruise in the small of his back made it more comfortable to lie on his stomach on the bed; anyway the back of his neck was so sore that even a pillow made it feel as though the leather was still cutting off his head.

How close he had come to death by the thong severing the nerves in that vital spot he would never know but as a testimony he would bear the white scar on his neck for the rest of his life.

Donahue thought that he was not by any means out of the woods yet. On the other hand there was now a chance that Petrov and his cohorts could be apprehended in Hawaii, providing Donahue could inform the right Authorities early enough. All he had to do was to reach America's newest island State without being pushed overboard one stormy night. He had no illusions about the fact that it would be him against the crew members of the *Vertaz*.

Obviously the most sensible thing to do would be to inform the Canadian captain of his position, perhaps even asking permission to use the radio. Against this was the possibility that he would be disbelieved — especially if Petrov had already told the captain some plausible story to counter any allegations made by Donahue as almost certainly he had.

There were twelve hundred miles to travel, slow miles by the look of the *Fraser*. Donahue reckoned they would be lucky to reach Hawaii in five days. If only he could radio Goddard in London,

Seven Nine could have people waiting. There was still the problem of informing the American authorities of Seven Nine's involvement in the whole Y181 business, but that was Goddard's job.

The attempted destruction of Zeus 5, prevented by Seven Nine, even though by accident, would surely be a big enough issue to overcome any petty feelings the American's might have about recent British activities in their country.

Ruefully Donahue wondered how on earth he could ever tell Goddard even half the story over a radio link; it would have to be coded and that would make it more impossible. There was more sense in attempting to contact Hawaii beforehand. However he couldn't very well send a message to the US base there without a full explanation of who he was — anyway, who would he send it to?

Donahue gave up thinking, relaxing as far as his bruise and neck allowed between the clean sheets of the bunk.

He kept a wary eye on the door.

The charming Professor Petrov and his colleague, the small smiling man, had introduced themselves to the captain at the earliest opportunity.

The Canadian was at ease as he spoke.

'More like one of those spy ships you mean,' said the captain.

Petrov looked amused.

He said protestingly, 'No, no — really Captain Simms, I cannot believe you really think that. The *Vertaz* was a genuine oceanographic survey vessel. Comrade Chkalov is a specialist in marine organisms whilst I have for many years interested myself in the peculiarities of the warm water current known as the Kuro Suwi.'

Captain Simms smiled across his luncheon table at his two Russian visitors.

'Look,' he said, 'I don't give a damn what your ship was or who, or what you are. The *Vertaz* is at the bottom of the Pacific now and I'm stuck with all of you until we berth at Hawaii. I just want to make it clear that there isn't going to be any trouble on my ship.'

Chkalov said. 'We all greatly appreciate your hospitality, Captain Simms but I do assure you that we are scientists and that our crew were manning a bona fide Soviet survey vessel.'

'Sure, sure — I understand.' Simms was still grinning.

Petrov said. 'There is one thing captain that we should tell you, it concerns the man Donahue, the one you rescued just prior to our departure from the scene of the accident.'

'The Limey you mean,' Simms asked, 'the one with the log round his neck?'

'Yes, the Englishman, I'm afraid it will be difficult for you to understand his presence on board a ship of the Soviet Republic.'

The captain said, 'Yeah,' waiting for Petrov to continue.

The small man Chkalov interrupted.

'Mr Donahue defected from the UK in nineteen sixty eight an entirely voluntary move as the word implies. He is, or rather was, a leading Western authority in oceanography and as such his experience was welcomed in the Soviet Union. This has been the second time he has made a trip in the *Vertaz*. Three weeks ago,

Mr Donahue suffered a most unfortunate accident falling several feet from a ladder during some rough weather. You will find that his right leg has a painful wound in the calf where it was injured by a protruding steel rod. At the same time he received a terrible blow on his left temple causing severe concussion. On recovery it was found that his mental faculties were impaired in some way. It appears that he believes that he is a Western agent acting for some spy organization.'

'A Seven Nine group,' said Petrov.

'Ah yes, captain, Seven Nine, the number of Mr Donahue's cabin. The *Vertaz*'s doctor, unfortunately lost with the ship, was unable to understand exactly what has happened to the poor man.'

'What a load of rubbish,' said Captain Simms good naturedly, 'I don't believe a word of it!'

Chkalov and the professor looked aghast.

Simms was close to laughter as he spoke.

'It's OK, it's your business. Maybe it's true. Sort it out after you leave my ship, that's all I ask. You guys kill me — have a drink.'

He passed a bottle across the table.

'Go on.'

Watching each other over their glasses the three men drank, each thinking his own thoughts.

After a few additional minutes of polite conversation on an unrelated topic the meeting broke up, Petrov and Chkalov retiring below to the spare cabin that had been found for them.

Captain Simms was not as big a fool as he appeared. He went straight to Donahue's cabin.

Still lying on his stomach the 'defected English scientist' squinted sideways at him.

Simms sat on the bunk.

'Your name Donahue?' he asked.

'Yes. Simon Donahue.'

'You a Limey scientist working for the Reds?'

'No,' said Donahue knowing his suspicions were confirmed.

'Then what were you doing on the *Vertaz*?'

Donahue rolled over and sat up. 'Will you believe me if I tell you?'

The captain said, 'I might.'

Rapidly Donahue decided how much he could disclose. The captain looked a reasonable man although beneath the skin under the eyes and web-like over the ruddy cheeks the thin red veins showed a hardened whisky drinker. A drinking captain is not necessarily an unreliable person to confide in — Donahue made up his mind.

'Firstly,' he said, 'I know that you've already heard one story from Professor Petrov. It isn't true but I appreciate that you can't take my word for that. I'm afraid my story will sound even less believable, nevertheless it's all true I swear. Only you can judge who is telling the truth. I hope for both our sakes you choose the right one.'

Donahue started from the very beginning.

It was to take the major part of the afternoon for him to recount all that had taken place since he had first been told of the Astra Physics sunseeker. It

186

seemed a long time ago since it had all started.

When he finished, throat dry from too many cigarettes and from talking, he turned onto his stomach again, waiting for the captain to speak.

'Hell,' said Captain Simms at length.

Donahue had one more thing to say.

'Whatever you think about what you've just heard, you must promise me that until you find out whether I've spoken the truth or not you must not mention a word of it to anyone.'

Simms said, 'And if it is true, I can tell anyone I like — don't be damned stupid.'

'You know what I mean,' Donahue said.

'Yeah, I know.'

Simms rose from the bunk.

'Hang on,' he said.

In a few moments he was back carrying the whisky bottle and two glasses.

'OK buddy,' he said holding out his hand, 'I'm with you.'

Donahue clasped it meeting the other's eyes.

There was silence as the two men drank.

'OK Mister Agent, what do we do now,' grinned the captain.

A dreadful fear suddenly gripped Donahue.

'The sub,' he breathed, 'I forgot the sub.'

Simms was out of the cabin before Donahue could explain properly.

His face was grim when he returned.

'Too late,' he said. 'And they smashed the radio.'

Donahue groaned.

He doubted that they would have radioed for help from the sub as other vessels might have been converging on the rescue area. Could they receive submerged? Surely they wouldn't attempt to raid the *Fraser* anyway. It would be impossible to take all the Russians on board the submarine but Petrov and Chkalov were the only two that mattered. There would be room for them.

'You'll have to change course, head back to Vancouver.'

'You must be joking Buddy.' Simms

was not amused. He stopped smiling.

Donahue explained the position.

'If they really want Petrov then they'll get him. And they won't risk an international incident of piracy, the chances are that the *Fraser* will vanish into thin air with you and me with it.'

Simms looked very worried.

'You don't know that's their plan,' he said. 'Perhaps they smashed the radio to stop any advance notice being given to Hawaii.'

Donahue said, 'No, I don't know, but we'd be idiots to take the risk wouldn't we?'

Simms said, 'Damn,' took a long drink from the bottle and said, 'Damn' again.

Donahue said, 'Good.'

He thought that returning to Vancouver might not save them, but the sub would have to surface to find them and in daylight too. They might have gone a long way to Hawaii before realizing their quarry had doubled back.

The dirty rust-streaked bows of the *Fraser* turned slowly away from the islands. Further and further they swung until the little freighter was on course for home.

In her hold, yet again, the canned fruit was turned about.

11

On July 14th, almost exactly at mid-day, the Zeus 5 capsule splashed down in the Pacific following a totally uneventful re-entry.

Although by now conditioned to space flights, the world greeted the safe return of the three astronauts with wonder and genuine relief. The mission had been entirely successful in every respect and, with the exception of a small number of Soviet politicians in Moscow and those Russians on board the *Fraser*, everyone was delighted.

There was a strained atmosphere on the Canadian freighter.

As the capsule floated gracefully down on her coloured chutes many miles to the south, the *Fraser* was within five hundred miles of Vancouver. She had been proceeding at best possible speed towards the Canadian west coast for the past three days and everyone on board was heartily tired of the whole trip already.

With the extra men from the *Vertaz*, conditions were cramped to say the least, whilst the incident of the smashed radio had created a general air of distrust bordering frequently on open hostility between Russian and Canadian crews.

Petrov and Chkalov, spokesmen for the Soviet contingent, had expressed surprise on receiving news about the radio.

It had been pointed out that there could be no possible motive for any of their men to have done such a thing, rather, they suggested, could it not have been the work of their unfortunate English colleague?

Captain Simms was advised to keep a careful watch on Donahue in order to safeguard the entire ship — unless of course he was prepared to let the Russians look after him as requested earlier.

Chkalov had made it clear to the captain that Donahue should be under the charge of Soviet officers as, to all intents and purposes, the man was part of their crew and hence their direct responsibility.

To this Simms had replied curtly that the scientist was very ill and that, as captain, he had no intention of letting anyone see him until proper medical aid was made available in Vancouver.

Donahue was locked in his cabin in order to protect him from any attempt on his life by the Russians, and to demonstrate that Simms believed him to be a potential danger to the ship.

From Donahue's point of view the confinement was not entirely satisfactory. He had spent too much time locked in tiny cabins of late. However, it did seem the only way for Simms to protect him at the same time as showing he believed the Soviet explanation of Donahue's condition.

In reality nobody believed anybody.

Donahue spent his time vainly trying to decide on what he should do should they manage to reach the Canadian coast in one piece. To avoid arousing further suspicion amongst the communists, he was only able to speak with Simms for brief periods during which both argued as to the best course of action to pursue.

Russians outnumbered Canadians making it an easy matter for them to take over the *Fraser* if they wished. Because of this, Simms had taken each of his men, making the position as clear to them as he could without leaking too much of the story that Donahue had told him.

The captain was a likeable man, not hard but not lax either. Although the crew of the *Fraser* could not be called a fine body of men by any stretch of imagination, they were tough and thought enough of Simms to stand solidly behind him in the event of any trouble.

And so, for the last seventy-two hours, Easterners and Westerners had moved warily about the *Fraser* keeping to their own kind, avoiding anything but essential contact.

Apparently inseparable, Petrov and Chkalov had meals with the captain, quickly learning to like the golden rye which, including breakfast, was part of every meal.

Donahue had wanted Simms to run without lights at night and to make small course changes whilst they were not obvious. Believing that both measures would be futile in attempting to throw off the submarine — if it was following — Simms had ignored the advice. Anyway, numerous ex-crew members of the *Vertaz* had developed the habit of taking a nocturnal stroll around the deck of the *Fraser*. To have no lights and to make course adjustments could only appear highly irregular to any competent sailor no matter what his country of origin.

If the submarine was to make a move, Simms reasoned it was likely that it would have been long before now — unless by some chance it hadn't caught up yet.

In brief discussions, Simms and Donahue had speculated on tactics should the sub materialize. Finally they had decided that all that could be done was to refuse to allow anyone to either board or leave the *Fraser*. If necessary, the *Fraser*'s crew was prepared to fight. Fight they would have to — against the Russians already on deck as well as any potential boarding party coming over the side.

Simms knew it would be a lost cause, but what else could they do?

Staring out from the bridge at the blue ocean, the captain of the Canadian ship thought of Korea.

That was the last time he had felt the same cold crawling in his body. The insidious creeping feeling when it's nearly over and you're nearly safe; that there's time still for you to get it but a chance you'll be one of the lucky ones.

Heart-leaping hopes that you're going to make it. Irrational hopes that if enough of your buddies get killed your chances are that much better.

Fear, stark fear, dispelled later by the smooth warm liquor pushing all of the whole rotten stinking mess of war far away into the dark.

It wasn't that bad yet but Simms wanted a drink.

He fought with the ache in his belly. He had a job to do. Not a job of great importance — not one that really mattered but still a job he could do right if he was still a man.

Maybe this one last time John Carter Simms could show himself that he wasn't a failure — not yet. Not a no-hoper captain with no future and without a need for one.

Just this one last time, he said to himself.

'Russell,' he yelled suddenly between cupped hands, startling a huge hulk of a man walking in front of the bridge.

'Come up here.'

Russell was the radio operator — when he had enough time.

'Sir,' he queried.

Simms said, 'Are you still sure it can't be fixed?'

'Hell Sir, you've seen it, a thousand little bits. Even if I knew where to start, it wouldn't do no good. I can operate a radio, that's all.'

In silence, Simms continued to stare out of the window.

The sea was less calm than of late, there was more of a swell but, in all directions, the sky was still cloudless as far as the horizon.

Perhaps, at this very moment, he was being watched through a periscope by the captain of another vessel: a killer sub floating unseen just beneath the surface.

He shivered in the July sunshine reaching for the comfort of the bottle.

In his cabin, Professor Petrov, late of the State Committee of Science and Technology, spoke quietly to Comrade Chkalov one of twenty-eight trained espionage agents, schooled for seven hard years to operate secretly in the United States.

Petrov was worried. The failure of his project would inevitably impair his reputation, not so much as a scientist in weapon control but his ability as an organiser would be necessarily suspect.

His presence on the *Vertaz* had been required for his technical capabilities in co-ordinating the checkout procedures for Y181. That he had been put in sole charge of the Zeus 5 'Shoot', as it was called in Moscow, was understandable but unreasonable.

Quite what his superiors would say, he dare not imagine.

Chkalov, on the other hand, had not failed in carrying out his assignment. Two years had been spent planning the eventual production of the two Y181 models. During this time the operation in the UK had been organized and the careful search in the States for suitable personnel had yielded Chuck and Ronald Curtiss — both American citizens.

The former had been employed at one time in the Aerospace Division of the Boeing Developmental Centre in Seattle as a Senior Engineer in the Flight Packaging Group. Chuck had held responsible positions on the 'Minuteman' and ill-fated Dyna Soar project before spending eight years running his own printed circuit board business in Burien, a suburb of Seattle.

Chkalov had approached Chuck knowing that his security clearance at Boeing had been suspect and that he was listed as having communistic leanings. The American's unusual and largely unsatisfied taste in small girls, coupled with strong sympathies towards the totalitarian system made him easy prey for the persuasive Chkalov.

Paedophilia — or the sexual desire for children — is usually a sign of an unbalanced mind. Chuck, when not absorbed by an engineering problem, lapsed into a fantasy land in which his personal shortcomings were mentally overcome by a variety of highly original physical and imaginary activities.

Chkalov was able to convince the engineer that power, and subsequent freedom to obtain satisfaction of any kind, could be easily found by assisting the cause of the Great Soviet Republic.

After working steadily for nearly six months, Chkalov finally won the battle over the mind of Chuck and the prototyping of Y181 could begin.

Curtiss had worked in the well equipped factory that Chuck had established, producing printed circuit board substrates on a sub-contract basis for the vast Boeing complex. He had been totally unaware of the work he was doing in San Carlos where he assisted in the assembly of the sun-seeking platforms, and he never asked.

Ronald Curtiss was a faithful servant to the Soviet cause without ever knowing.

Chuck, together with Curtiss and Chkalov had formed Guidance Systems to assemble and test Y181 in California. Now, both Americans were dead.

Comrade Chkalov thought that it was all very convenient. Chuck presumed drowned with the *Vertaz* and the fool Curtiss with the Englishman's hunting arrow in his back. He was moderately pleased with the way things had gone. Certainly the prototypes were lost, but the microfilm copies were in Moscow. There would be another opportunity.

The two Russians were concerned that no sign of rescue had yet materialized.

Coded messages should have been received by the submarine either directly from the *Vertaz* or subsequently by relay from Moscow.

Both men were sure that the sudden course reversal of the *Fraser* could not have confused the commander of the sub.

Actually Chkalov was rapidly regretting his instruction to destroy the radio on the Canadian ship. At the time there had been no need to use it to transmit information concerning the return of the *Fraser* to Canada. It would have been better not to have been so hasty.

The two men chatted quietly wondering whether it was now too late for them to be taken off the *Fraser*.

Petrov said, 'If we are taken to Canada we must make sure that all the men are aware of the cover story in great detail. It will be some time before we will be able to arrange transportation home.'

Chkalov nodded.

He said, 'Although it will be a nuisance to be questioned by the Western Authorities, I don't believe that we have anything to fear providing the English agent can be silenced beforehand.'

'But we think that the captain believes Donahue.' Petrov spoke with some insistance, he had been unable to convince Chkalov of this.

He continued, 'That means that they will both have to be quietened and we certainly can't do that without causing major trouble either on board or when we land.'

Chkalov said, 'So what do you propose my dear professor?'

Petrov's voice rose, 'We have been discussing this same problem now for two days. It would seem we may not be able to rely on the submarine and consequently will have to manage with our own wits. I would remind you Comrade that we are running out of time.'

'Really professor,' Chkalov replied. 'There is more than enough time to formulate an adequate plan.'

He smiled. 'We can always take over the ship as we discussed although quite what we should do then I cannot imagine. I'm sure we could never reach the USSR. Also it may be that the hunt for the *Fraser* is already on as obviously she has not acknowledged any radio communication since picking us up.'

Chkalov was close to laughter as he finished speaking.

'I will think of what we are to do Petrov — please leave everything to me.'

The professor was to regret taking this advice.

On July 13th the Canadian CL28 had taken off again from the tarmac strip at Air Sea Rescue headquarters on Midway Island.

This time it was daylight. Her mission was to seek and find the merchant vessel *Fraser*, believed en route from the scene of the *Vertaz* disaster to Hawaii.

Elated at his previous success, the captain flew on a straight course or, as he said continually — as the fly crows — from the Islands to the reference marked in red pencil on his map.

Astonished at discovering no trace of the *Fraser* he turned and flew a conventional search pattern, eighty miles wide, all the way back to ASR where he admitted shamefacedly to being unable to find any sign of the Canadian freighter.

The USAF were disturbed. ASR were accused of bungling. Bobby Antigo was removed in disgrace from duty, this being one positive move that the Air Force could make.

Just before the CL28 turned to

commence her search pattern, the navigator had announced loudly that there was a submarine below.

Hawaii expressed surprise at the radioed information but offered no specific instructions. By the time the aircraft had doubled back the sub had vanished causing the navigator to be unjustly accused of sensationalism and incompetence as an observer.

Just because the CL28 was a sub hunter didn't mean that it had to continually discover submarines. Anyway, it was known that the navigator had a plastic hip flask in the thigh pocket of his flying suit.

Nevertheless, there were thinking men on Midway Island. Men not hidebound by constraints imposed by a military way of life. The report of the possibility of a sub close to the spot where the *Vertaz* had sunk was interesting — even perhaps a little disturbing.

Whilst the Pacific Fleet was busily engaged in retrieving the Zeus 5 capsule, a restricted red alert went out to certain vessels of the United States Navy.

Information was scant, but enough uncertainty existed in the disappearance of two ships — one of them a Soviet Survey vessel — to create an air of slight suspicion.

As evening fell, speculation on the fate of the *Fraser* increased. By this time, as well as a group of civilians on Midway Island three North American bases were involved in considering what action should be taken.

That night, on board the *Fraser*, an attempt was made to kill Simon Donahue.

Earlier in the evening Simms had learnt more of Donahue's assignment in a long talk made easier by the trust that now had been established between them. Both men admitted to believing that they would reach port without trouble. In anticipation they discussed the arrangements that would be necessary for the arrest of the communist leaders.

As usual, when Simms left, he locked the cabin door behind him leaving Donahue comfortably full of rye.

The slow wallow of the *Fraser* lulled

him gently to sleep without knowing that he was even tired.

Afterwards Donahue could not remember what had caused him to open his eyes at that moment. Perhaps there had been a noise, perhaps enough of his training remained to keep part of his brain clear of the warm fog of the whisky.

On the inside of the door, the crude steel lever was creeping downwards.

In an instant he was on his feet, heart banging.

Donahue forced himself to be calm.

The door should be locked — all on board knew that. Whoever was outside would not be bothering to try the lever unless the lock had been freed first.

Behind the door he tried desperately to shake off the scales of sleep as he waited breathing softly.

It swung inwards.

Donahue waited until the shadow from the passage began to move. Using all his strength, bruised back against the wall and injured leg against the door, he heaved.

Three hundred pounds of steel accelerates

remarkably slowly.

The shadow moved back, but not quickly enough.

In throwing his body backwards to avoid the closing door, the leg of the man outside swung up and forwards into the rapidly closing gap. Even when pushed violently it takes a six foot door of steel a long time to close. When it does the stored energy is enormous.

The soft crunching of flesh and bone was accompanied by a long drawn out, 'Ahhhh' as the intruder's ankle was crushed to half its thickness.

On the floor, writhing in pain, lay one of the crew from the *Vertaz*. Beside him a short knife, with a heavily curved blade, shone dully. Donahue kicked it inside his cabin.

Two men arrived simultaneously — one from the cabin next to Donahue's — the other running down the passageway. Both were Canadians.

Donahue said, 'Quick, get him away from here before any Reds arrive and ask the captain to come down.'

One of the men, the big radio operator,

Russell, who had picked Donahue out of the water, grinned at the Englishman.

He said, 'That's the way buddy, don't you take no funny business from these guys.'

He picked up the Russian and began to drag him away, the other Canadian watching with a pained expression as the man's injured leg bounced along the deck plates.

Simms entered Donahue's cabin a few minutes later. He looked concerned.

'What the hell happened?' he asked.

Donahue tossed the knife to him.

'They finally had a go,' he said.

The Captain sat down heavily.

'How did they get in?'

Donahue said, 'Either they got a key or picked the rather rudimentary lock on the door. It's lucky I woke up in time.'

Simms said, 'You can say that again.'

Donahue retrieved the knife and put it under his pillow.

He said, 'You'd better get back up top in case there's trouble over this. I doubt if you'll hear anything about it though. I'll keep the knife.'

Simms said, 'I'll send Russell down for company,' leaving swiftly before Donahue's protests could begin.

The remainder of the night was uneventful, if Donahue could regard the loss of $67 to Russell in a long poker game as uneventful.

Later he managed to sleep for several hours with the big Canadian sitting on the floor, back against the door, drowsing.

As a bodyguard, the sheer size of Russell was very reassuring.

By morning, the sea which had been calm since Donahue had been taken from Cape Alvera, had become quite choppy. White caps were alternately whipped and smoothed by squally rain sweeping from the south.

Steadily the wind increased throughout the morning causing the little *Fraser* to wallow more than usual in the troughs moving slowly onto her starboard quarter. At eleven o'clock the rain stopped suddenly, improving visibility to about five miles.

From the south east, bearing down on the *Fraser*, semaphore flickering, the

United States destroyer *Defiance* was a magnificent sight.

On the bridge Donahue poured a large glass of yellow rye for Captain Simms and one almost as big for himself.

Below, the crew of the *Vertaz* had orders to report singly for briefing to Professor Petrov's cabin.

12

In the increasingly stormy sea, like a fat grey seal the *Fraser* ploughed happily onwards, her watchful guardian occasionally losing sight of her as she wallowed in a particularly deep swell.

Semaphore lights had told part of her story to *Defiance* during the afternoon of the 15th causing the destroyer to pass the message; 'Please alter course to San Francisco.'

To this the worthy captain of the *Fraser* had replied with commendable brevity, 'Get lost.'

A short pause had followed this signal.

Eventually *Defiance* sent; 'Will accompany you to Vancouver.'

Answered politely by Simms, 'Thank you.'

Rightly, Donahue assumed that the destroyer would relay all signalled information directly to both Canadian and United States security. Because of this suspicion it proved remarkably difficult to send enough facts to produce what he hoped to be a believable story without involving Y181.

He was very tired of not being able to use any authority in organizing what he knew should be done to guarantee that Petrov and Chkalov would be apprehended as soon as they entered Canadian territorial waters.

Donahue had not allowed Simms to refer to Y181 in any way; indeed it was only after a good deal of soul searching that he had convinced himself to tell the captain about the sunseeker at all. In order to explain his presence on board the *Vertaz*, it had been necessary to convey to Simms something of Donahue's assignment. He had made brief reference to a 'British device' and left it at that.

Although it had been a small and easy search, Simms and Donahue congratulated themselves on their good fortune in being the subject of a sea hunt by the United States Pacific Fleet. Fear of the submarine gave way to feelings that they had played their part in the cold war without letting down the side. Both men were relieved that help had arrived.

The remaining miles to Vancouver Island passed swiftly. Russians lining the shaky rails of the *Fraser* alternately watched *Defiance* on the starboard bow and the increasingly distinct line of the Canadian mainland looming ahead.

Squalls still swept across the deck of the freighter from time to time, causing visibility to fluctuate and drenching the men refusing to shelter below. A general air of excitement pervaded the ship. Russians and Canadians anticipated their arrival in Vancouver with very different feelings.

At last *Defiance* fell slowly astern of the *Fraser* as the rusty little ship passed Cape Flattery entering the comparative calm of the Juan-de-Fuca straits.

Fifty miles to the south, Mount Olympus was seen briefly in the clear swath of blue sky stretching down the entire length of the Olympic peninsula.

Watching this unusual sight Donahue realized that he was but a few miles from his point of departure from the coast. He wondered if his bow was still lying there in the mud.

What had happened to the burro? Was Chuck's Plymouth still parked at the beginning of the Alvera trail?

His whole trip seemed unreal. A voyage to the middle of the Pacific in one ship and back in another. And all in a few eventful days.

The escort destroyer blinked a brief farewell to her charge; from here onwards the *Fraser* would be safe. Soon other smaller vessels would be joining her for the final run past Port Angeles up to Vancouver.

More British than Britain, Victoria slid by gracefully to port. Donahue choked with memories. He remembered the flight from Seattle to Vancouver over the San Juans after killing Curtiss and recollected the tight knot in his stomach on that clear June morning.

One day, one day when it was all forgotten, he would return as he had promised himself. The girl with the soft fragrant hair by his side as together they would walk through the forests and explore the islands in the summer sunshine.

Donahue ached for Jane. So much had happened that now the brief night spent at Farnham was a lost sweet memory.

Seven Nine could manage without him. There wouldn't be a next time — not again — ever. Goddard could never be persuasive enough.

Donahue resolved not to forget the sick fear that had assailed him waiting to be caught in the engine room of the *Vertaz*.

His thoughts were interrupted by Simms shouting from the rail behind the small bridge.

'Simon — here.'

Followed closely by Russell, who still refused to move more than a few feet away, Donahue climbed to the highest and most important part of the *Fraser*.

Simms said, 'Over there.'

Ahead of them a Coast Guard Cutter, obviously from Sidney on the Saanich peninsula was turning into the Haro Strait.

The *Fraser* was bisecting the imaginary

line dividing Canada from the USA as Simms spoke. For six miles she would be in America before re-entering official Canadian waters.

Following the direction of the captain's finger, Donahue watched the green and white smartness of the fast patrol boat throwing up an even curl of white water each side of her sharp prow.

He said to Simms, 'I'll go on with them as we said.'

The captain nodded agreement. 'I still think Russell should go with you, Simon.'

Donahue didn't answer.

Three men from the *Fraser*'s crew clattered up the ladder and entered the glass-enclosed area where the captain and Donahue stood.

One of them said, 'That'll be the *Victoria Scout*, Sir.'

Simms replied, 'We're expecting a special boarding party Scott — it's funny she's by herself. Perhaps the Navy's too damn lazy to hoist anchor.'

Two hundred yards away they heard the trim launch throttle back as she approached the *Fraser*.

217

Simms gave the instruction to stop engines.

In a slow sweep the Cutter swung in an arc coming neatly alongside. By contrast, bright paintwork on the Coast Guard boat made the freighter appear dirtier than ever.

Permanently welded to the rust of the *Fraser*'s hull was a dangerously corroded ladder which, it was said, took over half a knot off her speed. No one had been able to convince Simms to have it removed. It was of untold value to the Captain when returning to his ship from local taverns on dark nights — much safer than other means of getting on board; and it was always in the same place.

To this the Cutter was tied, nestling quietly against the rusty side of the *Fraser*.

Simms said, 'You stay here until I get the Reds out of the way — no sense in taking chances at the last minute.'

Donahue could see Petrov and Chkalov leaning over the rail immediately above the Coast Guard launch. He felt strangely sorry for them.

Captain Simms turned to leave the bridge.

'Don't forget what I said,' he reminded Donahue.

Without warning, the harsh stammer of machine guns sounded on deck; simultaneously the port windows of the bridge shattered to a thousand pieces. Bullets whined through the metal roof.

Two of the men standing beside Donahue fell to the floor.

Simms, Russell and the other man dropped to join Donahue crouching on the floor. The bridge house was congested.

Simms said, 'God Almighty!'

There was some shouting on deck.

Donahue said, 'Keep your fingers crossed that all they want are Chkalov and Petrov, if they come up here we're dead men.'

Inside minutes there was a sudden roar from the engines of the cutter followed by another burst of fire from the machine gun — this time not directed at the bridge.

Through spears of broken glass Donahue

peered cautiously over the window edge.

Exhausts crackling, on full power, the launch was accelerating rapidly away in the direction from which she had come.

There was chaos on the deck of the *Fraser*.

Men were fighting from one end of the ship to the other.

Two rungs at a time Donahue ran down the steps shouting, 'Simms quick — we've got to stop this!'

Impressively the captain paused, a battered megaphone in his hand. His voice bellowed out over the *Fraser*, and over the waters of the strait.

'Enough you pack of bastards — enough!'

Slowly, one group after another, men stopped struggling.

'Stop!' yelled Simms through the megaphone.

Incensed at the attack on their ship the *Fraser*'s crew stood chests heaving, fists clenched glaring at the Russians who had seemed to be losing despite superiority in numbers.

The captain threw the megaphone onto the deck.

'Get some help up here,' he shouted, and descended to join Donahue.

In the distance the Coast Guard launch disappeared round a projecting headland leaving a thin line of white wake on the grey water.

There were no casualties on deck but it was unnecessary to ask; Petrov and Chkalov with three other Russians were gone.

Simms was bitter.

He said to Donahue, 'So much for the escort into port. What an incompetent bunch of idiots. A whole destroyer to Cape Flattery then nothing.'

He spat over the side.

Donahue was more disappointed than bitter. He was very glad to be alive. One of the two dead men on the bridge could just as easily have been him.

He said, 'Great isn't it? Half way across the Pacific probably shadowed by an enemy submarine, then we're fooled by a Coast Guard launch when we're within spitting distance of home.'

Alongside one of the life boats, sullenly, the remaining Soviet crew were gathering.

It was difficult to read their expressions.

Canadians moved slowly to their duties whilst the *Fraser* started to yaw in the channel under the slow but steady pressure of the current.

The captain gave the order to get underway, being interrupted by a disturbance in the bows where men were running excitedly back to the superstructure.

Someone shouted, 'It's coming back!'

Simms ordered, 'Engines full ahead. Everyone take cover.'

It was a false alarm.

Accompanying the Coast Guard launch was a veritable flotilla of other boats, one of them a frigate of the Royal Canadian Navy.

As the welcome party drew nearer it was possible to see that the launch was not the same one. Painted on its bows in gold letters was the name *Victoria Scout*.

Lining the rails, waving and jeering as the freighter cut her engines yet again, the men on the *Fraser* shouted a multitude of rude comments across the water to their fellow countrymen.

Minutes later the decks of the Canadian ship were smothered in officials from a variety of Government departments. White uniforms mixed with the drab blue sweaters of the seamen; men swarmed everywhere. Never had the *Fraser* been the scene of so much activity.

Eventually, Simms and Donahue extricated themselves from the melee together with three members of the party that had come on board and retired to the captain's cabin.

Initially there was confusion aggravated by the good captain who forcibly made it clear that he considered the whole business a disaster.

'A complete bloody fiasco,' he roared at no one in particular. Simms quietened after that and generous glasses of the inevitable rye soothed the gathering to the point where Donahue judged he could command some attention.

Lighting a cigarette he put his glass on the table and stood away from the assembled group.

'Gentlemen,' he said, 'my name is

Donahue. I represent the British Government — if you would be kind enough to introduce yourselves perhaps we could settle down and discuss this whole thing sensibly and quietly.' He was almost impressed by the speech himself.

There was silence.

He said, 'Right. You must already have some idea of who I am and what has happened but there is a lot you can't know yet. Before I explain anything you must know that five communist agents were taken by force from this ship only minutes ago by an apparently genuine Canadian Coast Guard vessel. Two members of our crew were killed during the raid.'

A distinguished officer from the frigate with much golden scrambled egg about his shoulders, snapped a command to his subordinate who rushed immediately from the cabin spilling Simms' drink as he pushed by.

More quietly, the officer drawled, 'Well, Mr Donahue, I guess we must have seen her as we came to meet you. Too bad your radio is bust or we'd've known. Maybe we can nail her yet, if she hasn't lost herself in the islands already. My name's Castledean — I'm sure glad to meet you.'

He held out his hand.

Castledean introduced the other man standing at his side.

'This is Mr Mansfield from Canadian Intelligence.'

After Simms had been formally introduced as well, Donahue went back to the beginning. He started by elaborating on the message sent to *Defiance* by the semaphore operator. Without interruption he recounted a suitably edited version of his assignment, making it clear that his timely intervention in preventing the launch of the Soviet missile was more accidental than intentional. Finally Donahue told of the very recent raid in which Petrov and the agent Chkalov were abducted — or rescued — depending on how you looked at it.

'What about the three other Commies?' asked Simms.

Castledean said, 'Probably scientists or engineers, Captain.'

Donahue nodded in agreement.

He said, 'I'm sure there must have been several other qualified engineers on the *Vertaz*; they couldn't possibly have operated a plan to knock down Zeus 5 using only Petrov.'

'It's quite a story,' Castledean said. He looked very impressed with what he had heard. 'You sure did a good job, Mr Donahue.'

Donahue asked, 'What about the Russians here on the *Fraser*?'

'Mr Mansfield will organize all that. Don't you worry about them.' Castledean smiled.

Mansfield, who until now had said nothing, swallowed the last of his rye and removed the jacket of his sombre suit. He was in his late forties running slightly to fat around the waist. Beneath his arms, sweat stained his shirt and small beads of moisture were standing out in clusters on his forehead. For July the weather was cool after the rain but as usual it was uncomfortably hot and stuffy in Simms' unventilated cabin.

With an extremely deep voice, surprising

the Englishman who had been expecting quite the reverse, Mansfield said —

'Mr Donahue, like Commander Castledean, I too am impressed with your apparent success in preventing a terrible event from taking place. I would be more impressed if I could believe all of it. However, I don't suppose for a moment that you can substantiate any of it or prove that you do in fact represent the British Government as you suggest.'

Donahue grinned, Mansfield was a more believable character than the commander.

'I rather thought Canadian Intelligence would have trouble in swallowing it,' he said.

Mansfield mellowed a trifle.

He said, 'In that case. I'm sure you'll be pleased to come back with me to my Department where we can talk some more.'

Donahue said, 'OK Mr Mansfield, I think that would be a good idea too. I can 'phone London from there and maybe clear the air a little.'

Simms asked, 'What about me?'

'I shall want to talk to you later as well captain — but not until you have berthed,' Mansfield replied.

Castledean said, 'Harry, why don't you and Mr Donahue hightail it right away. I can tie up all the loose ends here on the way in. I'll see you as soon as everything's all tidy on the *Fraser*. Tell your man Jackson what you want done with our Russian friends and I'll take it from there.'

Mansfield rose to his feet and put on his jacket.

'You ready?' he asked Donahue.

Simms said, 'I'll see you later Simon.'

Turning at the door, following Mansfield, Donahue winked at the Captain.

'I guess I owe you a few drinks,' he said, 'I'll be back as soon as things are sorted out.'

Climbing down the *Fraser*'s rusty ladder to the *Victoria Scout*, Donahue found that he had formed a surprising attachment for the little freighter that had rescued him from the sea.

He waved to Russell leaning over the side.

In the launch, drawing away from the four or five vessels surrounding the *Fraser*, he could see the broken windows and bright scars where bullets had sloughed off rust and white paint. Donahue sighed inwardly. Shortly he would be back on land.

He knew exactly what he was going to do. On the telephone almost certainly London would give authority for Donahue to collaborate fully with the Canadians.

Simon Donahue had always been sure that this would be the case but he could not afford to take the decision himself without first checking with Seven Nine in London. At last he should be able to get the whole story off his chest and let some other people do some work.

Engines quiet, the launch rubbed her smart white rope fenders along the concrete wharf at the end of the Coast Guard section of Vancouver quay.

Donahue spoke to Mansfield.

'Mr Mansfield. I imagine the signal from *Defiance* mentioned that I work for an organization called Seven Nine in London?'

A smile flickered transiently at the corners of the heavy jowls on the Canadian's face.

'One of Francis Goddard's bright young men,' he said.

Donahue was surprised.

'You know Goddard,' he queried.

'Yeah, for twenty years, I guess Mr Donahue.'

A black car was waiting for Mansfield, engine running.

It was better to be moving in the car than standing still or walking on land. Donahue wondered how long it would take him to get his land legs back.

Mansfield spoke, 'I won't save it for a surprise, there's someone waiting for you in my office right now — Goddard.'

Donahue was astonished. To have arrived in Vancouver so quickly his chief must have been notified as soon as *Defiance* met the *Fraser* and received the messages. Quite why he had found it necessary to meet him in Vancouver was a little mysterious Donahue thought.

Outside an unimpressive stone building the car drew up somewhere near the main city centre. Donahue didn't know where, he hadn't been looking where he was being taken.

For the first time in many days he became conscious that his clothes were a little odd.

Covering the bandage still round his neck, the polo-necked sweater he wore was grossly distorted giving the impression that he had no neck at all. An old pair of Simms' trousers which were much too short flapped annoyingly about his ankles.

Leaving the elevator Donahue became quite nervous.

'After you,' Mansfield waved him into his office.

Francis Goddard rose to meet Donahue.

The chief of Seven Nine stared at him for some time before speaking.

'Hello, Simon.'

'Hello, Sir.'

'A fine job Simon. The CIA and M4 have wanted Chkalov for over a year — and you've got this chap Petrov too.'

Donahue swallowed.

Goddard went on. 'I imagine Y181

sunk with the *Vertaz* which means I suppose that your assignment was successful. As you seem to have saved Zeus 5 from disaster as well I can only say that your performance has been splendid, even though most of it has been accidental.'

Mansfield said, 'The *Fraser* was boarded before she reached here by someone who got hold of a real Coast Guard patrol boat. Petrov and Chkalov are gone.'

Goddard slumped back into the chair behind Mansfield's large desk. 'Where to?'

Mansfield shrugged. 'They got three others too.'

Goddard said, 'Hell, what rotten luck.'

Henry Mansfield sat on his desk in front of Goddard.

'Francis, I brought Mr Donahue here to make sure that he is Simon Donahue.'

There was a snort from Goddard.

'That's him all right!'

The chief of Seven Nine realized he was being unnecessarily rude. 'Simon, I know it's not your fault. The old Y181 job seems to have expanded a bit. You did well — very well.'

He fumbled in a pocket.

'I've got a letter here from poor Marshall's sister — Jane, I think, her name is. I didn't know you knew her. She came up to the office for David's things just as I was leaving. Funny, she asked about you. Anyway she wrote this when I said I hoped to meet you here. Nice girl.'

Donahue took the envelope.

He said, 'I'd better tell you the whole thing before I forget any of it. Could you arrange a tape, Mr Mansfield?'

For the last time, or so he hoped, Donahue told of every detail he could remember, the others listening keenly as the spools turned lazily on the big recorder on the desk.

13

Goddard had arranged a hotel reservation for Donahue in Graham Street. It was conveniently near to the headquarters of Canadian Intelligence as well as handy to Vancouver's sprawling city centre. Goddard himself was the guest of Henry and Isobel Mansfield miles away on the east slope of the town.

On the bed in the hotel room, a complete set of clothing lay next to a new cordless electric razor, a green glass bottle of after shave lotion and a wallet containing two hundred dollars. Goddard had been especially thoughtful on this occasion.

Altogether it had taken four hours in Mansfield's office before all the questions had been asked and Donahue had learnt what there was to know about the agent Chkalov.

Before the formation of Guidance Systems in San Carlos, the Russian had been wanted by the CIA for his association with a known security leak from the Convair plant in Pomona. At that time, it had been established that a communist ring was operating in Northern California although it was not thought that a complete cell was yet in existence.

Three times the net had been closed and three times it had been empty. However, on the second attempt sufficient information had been disclosed to disrupt the chain of agents working inside Convair, and subsequent careful interrogation and sifting of statements revealed that the man Chkalov was the ringleader. That had been almost two years ago.

Eighteen months ago the CIA had passed the file on Chkalov to the Canadians in an attempt to widen the search. Canadian Intelligence and Seven Nine had been working together for the past year under the control of Goddard in London. Assistance had been volunteered by the CIA but politely declined by Seven Nine.

Recently, the pattern of events at the

beach house in Oregon and the seizure of the first Y181 model had seemed to indicate possible involvement of someone with the talent of Chkalov.

Now for the fourth time he had escaped.

Showering luxuriously, Donahue thought that the Russian agent must be very clever and very valuable: stealing a Coast Guard launch was a pretty desperate move, Moscow must think highly of their man to take such risks.

Mansfield had indicated that there was obviously still a chance that the escaped communists would be caught — civilian and military organizations had been mobilised early that afternoon. The tiny grass air strips, the float plane landing clearings on lakes and rivers throughout British Columbia, were all openly alerted by the extensive radio network operating in the wilderness of the North West. Rangers, fire wardens, traders and even trappers had listened to the terse instructions given over all frequences to watch for any suspicious movement of unrecognized small ships or planes.

The Coast Guard launch had been quickly found abandoned on the north coast of Swartz Bay opposite Piers Island, but there was no evidence to show the fate of the crew or indicate what means of transport had been used from there onwards, although it was universally believed that a light amphibian would have been an obvious choice. By now, the Russians could be comfortably camped anywhere in the vastness of the Canadian forests and lakes.

The telephone rang.

Donahue padded wetly from the shower across the carpet to the table.

'Simon?'

It was Goddard.

'I forgot to tell you, Mansfield's arranged for a doctor to see about your bumps and bruises at 8 o'clock this evening.'

Donahue said, 'Oh', adding, 'thanks but the leg's perfectly OK and the neck is only stiff now.'

Goddard said, 'Well it's all arranged and it can't do any harm to have yourself looked at can it?'

He went on, 'Simon, I'll see you in the morning at Mansfield's office — we want to have a quick look over the place at the Cape just in case there's anything that might help. Henry has arranged an Iroquois so it won't take long.'

Donahue thought that it would be a wasted trip.

He said, 'I'll be there at nine.'

Goddard rang off before Donahue had time to remove the receiver from his ear.

He walked to the bathroom for a towel and returned for a cigarette.

The phone rang again whilst he fumbled with a wet match.

It was the receptionist.

'Mr Donahue, there's a doctor to see you.'

Donahue said, 'Send him up, please.'

Still naked, leaving wet footprints all over the suite, he slid the safety chain from the door.

He lit another match.

A discreet knock sounded on the door.

'Come in,' shouted Donahue throwing his sodden cigarette into the ash-tray with disgust.

At the sound of the closing door he turned, finding to his utter dismay an attractive young woman looking amusedly at him from the entrance.

'Mr Donahue?'

Donahue grabbed his towel.

'I'm Doctor Hughes,' she smiled, 'I appear to have interrupted your shower.'

Simon Donahue fled.

When he came back, fully clothed, the doctor had lit a cigarette of her own, the smile still crinkling the corners of her wide mouth.

'I didn't think doctors smoked in this enlightened age,' Donahue said: he felt embarrassed.

'Patient therapy,' she replied shortly, 'I'm told you have a bullet wound in your leg and a deep cut in your neck.'

Donahue grunted. He leant forward exposing the weal on the back of his neck. The shower had made it sting.

'And the leg?'

He pulled up a trouser leg, 'It's OK now.'

With cool fingers she probed the puckered dimples each side of the calf.

'You were lucky.'

Donahue said, 'It could've missed altogether.'

'Part of the cut on your neck is infected — I shall have to clean it I'm afraid and give you an injection, Mr Donahue.'

'Call me Simon.'

His embarrassment was forgotten.

'Please keep still!'

Expertly she cleansed the deep groove and applied a new crepe bandage.

'Bare your arm please Mr Donahue.'

'Simon.'

Donahue hardly felt the needle.

Swiftly the leather bag was repacked, the unsmoked cigarette smouldering in the ash-tray was stubbed firmly out and Doctor Hughes was ready to leave.

She said, 'You were even luckier with the leather cut.'

Donahue asked, 'How do you know about that?'

She paused, hand upon the door: the faint smile appeared again. 'Henry Mansfield is my father, 'Mister' Donahue — Good-bye.'

★ ★ ★

By nine thirty he had eaten far too well in the Hotel dining room and consumed four cans of excellent cold beer.

He undressed slowly, climbed into the middle of the double bed and opened Jane's note.

It was very brief, she had not had time to write a proper letter.

Reading the familiar neat writing, Donahue remembered his thoughts of earlier in the day. He sniffed the paper but could detect nothing of the girl, it smelt of Seven Nine.

He switched off the light.

★ ★ ★

The squally rain of the day before had passed leaving the morning clear and warm as the three men drove from the city to Vancouver's International Airport.

'Not a trace,' Mansfield had answered Donahue's first question. 'Perhaps today though — I shall remain at Headquarters in case of any news. I'll let you know by radio if we hear anything.'

Gas turbine shrieking at the pitch which never failed to set Goddard's teeth on edge, the olive green Iroquois was waiting for them two hundred yards away from the passenger building.

Even though both knew the rotor was many feet above, the two men ducked instinctively as they approached the helicopter. They waved to Mansfield from the door.

'Better buckle up,' the young pilot pointed to a pair of rudimentary aluminium seats bolted to the floor behind him.

Donahue had only been in a 'chopper' once before; he had forgotten the noise and sudden lift off.

He grinned at Goddard who was looking terrified watching the ground falling away beneath them at a tremendous rate.

The flight to Cape Alvera took sixty-five minutes.

Several times had Donahue traversed this small part of the American continent. He had walked some of it, driven over part of it, sailed away from the coast — sailed back past it and was now flying over the rain forest.

From the air he was surprised to find that the actual trail could be picked out easily.

The pilot brought the chopper down gently in the little grass clearing between forest and beach, the down draught scattering leaves and small pieces of driftwood around them in a huge circle.

The silence was marvellous.

Thankfully, Goddard stepped down onto the springy grass still glistening with morning dew.

'I'll stay by the radio, Sir.' the pilot poked his head out of the sliding window above the hatch.

'That's it,' Donahue pointed to the Indian cabin expecting it magically to have somehow changed since he had been here last.

'Hang on a minute Sir.'

He trotted a short distance back towards the dark green of the trees and bent down into the grass.

He waved the black bow at Goddard. 'I hoped you'd lost it for good,'

Goddard snorted when Donahue rejoined him.

Donahue looked pained.

'It's done a lot of work for Seven Nine,' he said, 'Work that couldn't be done by anything else — you know that!'

Goddard ignored him as they walked towards the tiny grey shack.

Donahue was wiping dew from the glassfibre.

'It's a Super Kodiak, two hundred dollars worth.'

He paused to unstring the graceful weapon. 'I'm glad to have it back.'

The door hung open.

Inside the cabin nothing had changed. The pile of empty cans was still there, so was the little propane cooker standing at one end. If he hadn't have known, Donahue would have said that the place had been unoccupied for months.

'Not much to see,' Goddard commented.

Donahue said, 'What did you expect.'

He pointed to a dark stain on the compacted earth floor.

'That was me.'

Goddard asked, 'Did they take everything?'

'As far as I could tell, I wasn't feeling very observant.'

Goddard kicked the pile of cans. Some were beginning to rust in the salt air.

'Waste of time coming,' he said gruffly.

Donahue grinned across the shack at him.

'I got my bow back.'

The pilot appeared at the door.

'Vancouver wants you, Mr Goddard,' he said.

Donahue said, 'Good news, maybe.'

They walked back to the helicopter.

The static was very bad. Goddard looked pained as he tried to listen, ear pressed hard against the earphone of the headset.

After a little while he handed the instrument to the pilot.

'I can't make out much of it,' he said.

'We're real low here Sir,' the pilot excused his equipment. 'Perhaps if I took her up a bit.'

Goddard said, 'We'll go on back

anyway — they couldn't say much over the air without half of British Columbia picking up the message.'

It was presumed that Chkalov would be monitoring all the radio signals that he could, providing that he had a receiver. From yesterday's general alert, the Russians must already know that the entire Province was on the look-out for them.

Once they were airborne again Donahue shouted across at his chief.

'Do you want to bother with the car?' he pointed downwards to a clearing. Three cars were parked at the side of the small lake that headed the beginning of the trail. One of the cars was the Plymouth.

Goddard shook his head. 'That's probably Mansfield's men there now,' he mouthed.

Donahue enjoyed the flight back to the air terminal — he thought that helicopters could save you a lot of trouble.

A driver from Canadian Intelligence met them on the apron. He passed Goddard a long white envelope with a red adhesive label on the flap.

It was a note from Mansfield, written on the most official note paper Donahue had ever seen.

It said:

'Unconfirmed report from Queen Charlotte Islands of two float planes landed Hecate Strait 7 p.m. yesterday, purpose of visit unknown. Will try and detain but have serious doubts as to success of this. Can Donahue arrange to leave at once in case identification proves necessary? signed: Mansfield.'

In spidery handwriting beneath followed:

'No other information of any kind has come to hand so far — I have a hunch this one might be worth chasing. I know Simon needs a well earned rest but someone has to be there who can definitely recognize Chkalov. I'm sure you can persuade him. The helicopter is at his disposal.'

It was signed Henry.

Donahue was grinning delightedly.

Goddard said, 'It looks as though they're going to try and go across the Aleutians.'

Donahue shook his head, 'Why not over Alaska, hop across the Bering Straits and they're safe — it's not all that far.'

The helicopter pilot joined them.

'I've been told by Flight Control to report to Mr Donahue for further orders,' he said, obviously pleased.

'Can you find the Queen Charlottes?' Donahue smiled.

The Canadian grinned back. 'If I follow the coast we should be OK Sir,' he said. 'We'll need a little while to get fuelled up though — twenty minutes say.'

Donahue walked back to the terminal building with Goddard.

He said, 'I wonder if it is them?'

Goddard wasn't sure, but then as he was continually reminding himself, he was a shocking pessimist.

After his chief had left, Donahue shut himself in a phone booth where he busied himself in the yellow pages for a few moments before making two short calls into town.

Then he thrust some dollar bills into the hand of one of the taxi drivers lining the sidewalk outside the building and gave brief instructions.

Twenty-five minutes later the driver met Donahue as arranged, in front of the Air Canada counter, handing him a parcel.

More bills changed hands and Donahue was sprinting for the helicopter.

'Let's go,' he shouted heaving himself through the hatch.

With coarsening pitch, the characteristic chopping noise began as sagging rotor blades straightened.

Faster and faster they whipped. Donahue could smell the burnt kerosene swirling about them.

The small wheels of the Iroquois left the ground, paused transiently a few inches above the tarmac then shot forwards and upwards.

Watching the terminal dwindle in size beneath him for the second time that morning, Donahue unwrapped the paper from his parcel revealing a long stout cardboard tube. Taking great care to avoid the wicked razor heads, lovingly he withdrew four brand new Magnum hunting arrows.

14

Whilst the Iriquois flew north over the coastal waters of British Columbia, Mansfield and Goddard waited patiently at the centre of the miniature communication network that they had created.

With the very limited resources at his disposal, Henry Mansfield had done what he could. For a large country, Canadian Intelligence is a small organization understandably concentrated in the more densely populated areas of the eastern cities. It's headquarters are in Ottawa.

Mansfield had moved from Montreal to Vancouver four years ago at his own request. He had a reputation for thoroughness but was regarded as an unimaginative person in his job which allowed his transfer to be processed without hindrance. In BC there was little enough for Mansfield to do which he found an entirely satisfactory state of affairs. He suffered from a heart condition.

Now, annoyingly, he was presented with a bigger task than he had ever encountered in the east.

Four men from his department had left by air for Ketchikan, just north of the Queen Charlottes where light aircraft would ferry them to Nechako in the western island chain. There a boat was waiting.

Donahue — undoubtedly a capable man in Mansfield's estimation, was already on his way in the helicopter whilst two Rangers had been instructed to prevent the planes leaving the area at all costs.

Mansfield hoped he had cast his net wisely. It was impossible to obtain wider coverage in this Province of Canada, especially when there was no guarantee that he had found the right prey. At any minute, other suspicious aircraft could be located elsewhere.

He sweated in his hot office.

Francis Goddard irritatingly clicked his ball point pen. Since returning from the Cape, he had drawn eight pages of asymetrical doodles which had failed to calm his nerves as much as usual. Unconsciously he felt that the present situation was being handled too loosely but was frustrated to find that he had no concrete proposal to offer Mansfield.

He said. 'God, Henry, I hate this sort of waiting.'

His friend smiled at him. 'Rather be with Donahue?'

'Not in that thing thanks!'

One of the six telephones that overnight had been moved into Mansfield's office rang noisily.

The Canadian answered it roughly. 'Well read it out man — go on.'

He listened.

'OK Keith — no — I'll let you know.'

The receiver slammed down.

'It's them all right,' he said, 'They just shot a Ranger — with a machine gun!'

Goddard waited.

Mansfield lit a cigarette.

'Vancouver Ranger headquarters just received a message from their Prince Rupert Station on the mainland, opposite one of the smaller un-named islands of the Queen Charlotte group. It was from one of the guys who first saw the planes. A pair of them went out in a boat first thing this morning to find out whether it was the Russians or not.'

Mansfield shook his head as if to show his disapproval.

He continued, 'They were told to keep away by a man standing on one of the floats. The fools said they were Canadian Rangers with orders to prevent the planes from leaving. They didn't stand a chance.'

'They machine-gunned the boat?' Goddard queried.

Mansfield said, 'Yeah. One guy swam for it. He got half his cheek shot away for his trouble.'

He picked up a phone.

He said, 'Tell the chopper that the target is OK, and get word to Trevor Sand to be careful.'

Goddard said, 'What the hell are they doing landing there anyway?'

Mansfield sucked noisily on his cigarette.

He said, 'Ranger said there was an oil or gas slick on the water, maybe one of the planes is in trouble.'

Yet another of the telephones rang.

Mansfield listened. He put his hand over the mouthpiece. 'Planes were chartered in Oakland — California,' he whispered to Goddard, 'American pilots.'

He grunted several times and said, 'Thank you Jackson,' before replacing the instrument.

'Do you think they still have American pilots?' Goddard asked.

The Canadian shrugged.

'Probably not — unless you call American Communists American. Whoever's behind this escape planned it pretty well when you think how little time they had. There were at least four men, maybe five, on that Coast Guard launch — I'll bet you a pound to a pinch of salt that they all come from south of the border.'

'Shouldn't we try and find the original pilots?' Goddard said, knowing in reality that there was little point.

Mansfield stood up stretching. His shirt was wet.

'I guess we should Francis, and we could try and find out who chartered the aircraft too, but it's not going to help is it? We know there's probably nine communists including Chkalov and Petrov up coast from here. They're armed, dangerous and obviously pretty damned smart. All we have to do is catch them before they take off again. Finding out what's gone before isn't going to help us much at the moment.'

Goddard said, 'Right, let's catch them then!' There was a hard ring to his voice. 'Can you get an Airforce fighter Henry?'

Mansfield looked uncomfortable. 'Yeah, I could.'

'If those planes take off, most likely we'll lose them forever,' Goddard stated fact.

Now he was on his feet too.

He leant across the desk towards the fat man. 'Come on Henry, what are we going to do?'

Mansfield reached for the red phone.

When he had finished speaking he looked at the Chief of Seven Nine and said 'Well, what do you think Francis?'

Goddard was still hard. 'If there's time it might work but you'll need to get more people up there.'

Mansfield answered quickly. 'If there isn't time there isn't time to get a fighter up there either. If they get off the water then we can call in the Airforce, but you'll have nobody to question Francis — not that way.'

★ ★ ★

The chopper was too slow after all. After some time in the cockpit alongside the pilot, Donahue realized with frustration that the forward speed was a good deal slower than any other aircraft he had flown in. But still, he thought, I suppose you can't have everything.

At two-thirty, whilst he was eating smoked meat sandwiches thoughtfully provided by Flight Control, the signal from Vancouver was received. They were instructed to fly directly to Nechako Bay. Donahue had never heard of the place.

The pilot explained that as far as he

knew it wasn't really a place at all — just a patch of grass on the west shore of one of the islands a couple of miles from the mainland. He wondered why they had been told to report there.

At five o'clock, nearly five hundred miles north of Vancouver, the Iroquois landed on the barren air strip. Two red Beachcraft Bonanza's were parked by a crude wooden building flanked by piles of fuel drums.

Four men ran across the grass; all carried rifles.

Donahue strung his bow shouting, 'Keep the thing going!' to the startled pilot.

'No stop it,' he ordered a moment later opening the door.

He dropped easily to the ground.

'Are you guys from Vancouver?' he asked.

One of the men made signs that showed he couldn't hear what Donahue was saying.

They hurried away from the noise of the helicopter to talk.

When the pilot joined them a few

minutes later, Donahue explained quickly.

'The float planes are still there, it looks like one of them has some sort of trouble. They killed a Ranger this morning.'

He waved a hand at the four men.

'All these guys are from CI; we've been told to make sure that the aircraft don't get away. We've even been told how to do it.'

Above the bandage Donahue's face cracked into a smile.

'These guys have a coded message from Vancouver for us. Tell the pilot Mac.'

All four men wore traditional Canadian hunting jackets and looked tough and fit. Their leader said, almost apologetically, 'We've been told to load the 'copter with fuel drums and drop them on the float planes.'

He couldn't help a grin.

Donahue was laughing.

He said helplessly, 'Come on then, let's load up our bomber.'

He addressed the pilot. 'How many can we carry?'

One of the Canadians answered, 'We

can't lift the fifty gallon ones but there's a few ten gallons, the little black ones.' He pointed.

Whilst the cargo bay of the Iroquois was stacked with the drums, each weighing over sixty pounds, Donahue spoke with Trevor Sand — one of Mansfield's men who had flown up earlier to Ketchikan. His team, Bill Fry, Otis Corder and Graham Nelson comprised two-thirds of Henry Mansfield's entire force.

Sand was obviously worried about the whole plan.

He said, 'You'll have to hover to drop the drums, with machine guns they'll fill you full of holes in two minutes.'

Donahue picked up one of the rifles, a fine lightweight Savage 99F.

He said, 'Not with these around they won't.'

Sand shook his head. 'I've been told no killing.'

Donahue's good humour evaporated. 'We're not playing Boy Scouts,' he shouted. 'These guys have shot at least three Canadians in the last two days, before that they had bigger and better ideas that would make your hair stand on end. There are only two men out there that are important — they won't be the ones using machine guns. As soon as you see anyone with a gun on those planes — start firing!'

He calmed slightly.

'If you don't, and if we're still in the air, I'll drop a drum on you.'

Sand seemed unsure, he didn't smile.

He said, 'A helicopter might be pretty difficult to hit from a float plane when you think about it.'

Donahue said, 'Yes it might, and it'd be a damn sight more difficult if someone's firing a rifle at you.'

He climbed into the Iroquois between the piles of oil drums.

He said to Sand. 'Get yourself into gear or I might have nothing to bomb. You said you can get within three hundred yards of the planes from the beach. We'll give you an hour to get into position — exactly.'

Sand made up his mind: he looked at his watch.

'OK — let's go,' he said to his soiled

and exhausted companions staggering with the last drum.

'We'll take the boat most of the way,' he said to the Englishman, 'and we'll cover you when you arrive.'

'At three hundred yards — I'll be lucky!'

Their eyes met: they understood each other.

Donahue looked at his watch as they moved away, nearly five forty-five, there wasn't going to be too much light. Maybe the planes wouldn't even try to take off now until tomorrow — if, of course, they hadn't gone already.

'Phil,' he shouted to the pilot who was relieving himself in the grass against a solitary fuel drum, 'we do our first run at six-forty.'

He thought he must sound like a World War Two bomber captain; the idea was faintly amusing.

He couldn't rest. He strung the bow, wandering idly around the perimeter of the grass knowing that with only four arrows he dare not squander one on target practice. A proper razor head is only good for one shot.

Donahue knew he was frightened again.

He'd only travelled north in case he was needed to identify a Soviet agent. Now here he was about to roll oil drums out of a helicopter into the teeth of machine gun fire. Why the hell he hadn't the sense to get one of Mansfield's men to do it he couldn't imagine — it had never crossed his mind he realized. That was the trouble, he thought bitterly, part of it's pure habit after a while.

He returned to the helicopter and began to discuss the job.

'It depends how well we get on,' he said, 'We'll start high and come down.'

The pilot was lying on his back chewing grass.

'How about a flying run? — It's worth a try and it'd be a lot safer.'

Donahue looked at his watch. 'There's just time for a practice drop, Phil.'

The pilot shook his head lazily.

'I'm wrong, neither of us'll learn anything from one run,' he said, 'you need hundreds.'

Donahue said, 'It may be better to start off with a real low drop, that way they may hold off firing because they don't know what we're up to. Once I've unloaded a drum they'll know we're dangerous.'

Phil squinted at him.

'You know as well as I do they're going to shoot first off,' he said.

Donahue went quiet.

They took off from the desolate clearing ten minutes early. Phil flew his one man crew and armament out to sea for a short while, 'to see the sun go down,' he said to Donahue.

Soon it was time.

Sand had described where the two aircraft were moored just off shore from the west coast of the island in a small bay. Like two white dragonflies at rest in the darkening shadow of the island they swam into Donahue's vision. He touched Phil's shoulder.

Both men donned intercom headsets and fixed their throat microphones whilst the pilot trimmed the helicopter, trying as far as possible to align the Iroquois with her burden directly over the little white crosses on the water.

'I'm going down now,' announced Phil, 'You tell me what you want from now on.'

Donahue slid open the wide cargo doors in the side of the fuselage; he had no idea when to start rolling out the heavy drums. Maybe he'd kill Chkalov with the very first one, he thought.

Mansfield had thought of this too. The chances of a direct hit on the cockpit, even from a stationary helicopter, were so remote that he had discounted the possibility at once.

At Phil's suggestion, a nylon cord was tied round Donahue's waist and firmly knotted to a cleat on the bulkhead. He could see why now. The downward blast of air past the doorway made him sure that he would be immediately sucked out if he ever dared to let go with his arms.

He looked down.

Phil was flying the Iroquois backwards, he had over-corrected for a slight breeze coming from the west.

Donahue kicked out two drums, watching them drift downwards becoming smaller and smaller until the black paint merged with the grey sea.

Bright flashes stabbed from the sides of each aircraft long before the expanding white spots showed where the drums had hit the water.

'Useless, bloody useless,' Donahue yelled, 'and they're shooting!'

He felt strangely removed from the danger of the guns flashing beneath him. Perhaps it was the lack of noise.

Phil was shouting in his earphones, 'Which way, which way?'

He said, 'Left and down,' readying two more drums.

The splashes must have been over one hundred and fifty yards from the two planes. He would have to do much better this time.

Two flashes from the shore distracted his attention for a moment. He remembered that Sand and his men were helping.

Donahue rolled the second two drums out.

The helicopter was a lot lower now,

he could see them fall all the way.

One was going to hit the tail — it landed disappointingly yards away in a spreading flower of foam.

Phil said, 'Not bad — try another two.'

Manoeuvring the drums was exhausting work. When he next looked, the planes were separating, one leaving a short wake behind.

Phil had brought the helicopter down too low.

Bullets chopped through the floor each side of Donahue. Kerosene spurted suddenly from the drums.

'Up,' he yelled. 'Up — Up.'

He pushed three more drums out without knowing or caring whether they were above the remaining stationary aircraft.

The Iroquois slid sideways as she climbed, throwing Donahue to his knees into pools of oil forming on the floor of the cargo bay.

There were no more bullets.

He peered over the door sill. The plane that had been moving was stopped, the other was only half a plane.

'Phil we got one!' he shouted.

It was impossible to tell how many of the drums had hit the aircraft but the rear of the fuselage was obviously smashed completely.

He had four left.

'Come on Phil — the other one,' he cried.

Donahue climbed forward.

The pilot shook his head weakly. A dark stain was spreading across a tear in the green flying jacket under his right armpit.

'Buckle in,' he instructed Donahue.

Sickeningly the helicopter tilted, the pilot heading for the dark edge of the mainland where a light strip indicated the presence of a small beach.

On the water, the float plane that had been taxiing had moved back to her stricken companion.

Donahue could see men climbing over the wings as the pilot swept the Iroquois in a low dive towards the beach. Thankfully there was no gunfire from the Russians.

Phil landed the helicopter rather like a light plane. Oil drums flew violently around the cargo area, luckily inflicting no major damage either to the aircraft or to Donahue.

Half in the water, half on the tiny beach, the helicopter sat at an unpleasantly dangerous angle with driftwood jammed in a solid mass between the primitive undercarriage. The Canadian cut the turbine, turned to Donahue and slumped suddenly in his seat.

Simon Donahue clambered awkwardly into the cockpit swearing under his breath. An overpowering smell of oil from the punctured drums reminded him of the moments spent in the engine room on the *Vertaz*.

Withdrawing the small sheath knife the Canadian wore strapped to his flying boot, Donahue hacked furiously at the nylon webbing of the pilot's harness.

He lay the unconscious man gently across the seat and unzipped the jacket. Where the pilot's shoulder should have been a jagged hole gaped open, proving on closer inspection only to be where a substantial chunk of flesh had been peeled back from the chest. Donahue had no idea how it could have happened.

The first aid kit was more comprehensive than he had hoped for, it even included a small handbook which Donahue consulted. He sprinkled a liberal quantity of sulpha powder into the wound and strapped a sterile pad tightly on the chest of the unconscious man. The flying jacket was saturated in blood.

His eyes caught a broken tubular strut swaying slightly with the vibration of the slowing rotor. He thought that one of the bullets must have shattered the aluminium tube causing the end to whip viciously across the pilot's chest.

Donahue picked up the radio, managing to raise Vancouver immediately. He gave a brief account of the present position and indicated that the helicopter pilot was in serious need of attention, adding that he was uninjured himself.

A mile from the shore the remaining amphibian was on the move again, going too slowly to take off.

Donahue watched it through the dusk.

They were going to beach it he realized suddenly — maybe only a couple of miles north on the mainland.

Once it was out of sight he switched on the helicopter's navigation lights finding rather to his surprise that they functioned without the engine running.

He retrieved his bow and the new arrows, jumped lightly onto the coarse sand from the shore side of the helicopter and began walking.

For the first time in a long while, Simon Donahue was in his own element fully armed. Suddenly he had become very dangerous indeed.

15

Softly and sensuously, darkness enveloped the shore bringing the calm of the unruffled water to the foot of the forest where Donahue was walking. Here and there a cricket began to chirrup heralding the welcome protection of the night to those living things that were just awakening. An occasional bird, late in finding a suitable roost, fluttered in the scrub on the foreshore. Quietness crept across the land.

He was certainly not dressed for a night hike along one of the most desolate shorelines in the world. Although Goddard had provided casual shoes in a moccasin style, they were not the genuine article and were performing in an appropriately awkward manner. The remainder of his kit was just about acceptable although the brown of his sports shirt was perhaps a little too light he thought.

He toyed with the idea of removing the bandage from his neck — but there would be time for that later.

Donahue had no choice but to follow the coast northwards, hoping that there would be no river estuaries or cliff faces between him and the seaplane. It was possible that his route might be excessively long, but in the dark, without map or compass, there was no other practical way for him to choose.

Unfortunately there would be less than half a moon and this would not be high enough to be of any benefit until well after midnight. He had two choices. Either carry on as he was now, moving painfully slowly over the rocks and the accumulated debris of branches and logs using sixth sense more than ordinary vision, or wait for the moon to rise.

As there was no way of knowing what geographical obstacles he might encounter, Donahue decided to press on, but at a sensibly cautious rate; after all, he had until morning to reach Chkalov.

Reducing anger still welled in his throat but, since leaving the Iroquois, inwardly his resolution had hardened to one of icy hate. Donahue had taken enough from these men. In the last few days he had seen good Canadians die for a quarrel not of their own making and his personal involvement in the whole assignment had, up to now been almost entirely passive. It was time for Simon Donahue to begin earning his money.

If he had bothered — or been able to analyse his feelings he would doubtless have been utterly astonished to learn that in reality this was the Donahue that Seven Nine employed.

Goddard knew full well that once his man had slipped into this particular mental condition he was virtually unstoppable, even perhaps invincible. The versatility, cunning, imagination and cold ruthlessness that possessed Donahue made him so dangerous at these times that if Goddard had known, he would have felt sympathy for the stranded Russians.

Unfortunately, circumstances rarely built up to the point where Donahue became this different man. More usually he exhibited no more than an average performance in the field. Now, Seven Nine, if they could have been aware of the transformation, would be able to wait with quiet confidence — their man was working well.

★ ★ ★

A little less than two miles north of the archer, the lonely group of Communists worked frantically on their solitary amphibian using the inadequate illumination of two cheap cigarette lighters.

After a promising start to the escape, things had turned sour. Understandably, under the circumstances, Comrade Chkalov had become most scathing.

On July 15th, Chkalov's successor Comrade Turinsk had alerted four Soviet agents permanently domiciled in California. Turinsk, a young enthusiastic graduate from the Soviet training school at Omsk, had been in the continental United States, living in San Diego, for twelve days. He had picked up the messages from *Defiance* using extensive Japanese communication equipment recently installed at his flat.

Eager to demonstrate his abilities, he had immediately taken precautions to ensure that Professor Petrov and his colleague Chkalov would not fall into Western hands.

If he had known of the submarine, it is entirely probable that he would not have bothered. As it was, a suitably imaginative plan was formulated and rapidly implemented.

It was a simple matter for him to contact those agents currently working in the fertile fields of Northern California's Aerospace industry. All were part of the disbanded Convair cell.

Turinsk experienced no trouble at all in chartering the float planes, using them to fly his men to the cover of the San Juan Islands. There the innocent pilots had been murdered. The Russian was a very practical young man.

He had been unconcerned with the fact that the aircraft were easily traceable; by the time the stupid Americans came to their senses it was expected that the party would have crossed the Bering Strait.

It was a daring plan on a grand scale. By sheer misfortune things had not turned out as planned.

At about the time that the *Fraser* bade farewell to the United States destroyer escort, Turinsk had been presented with an unexpected piece of luck. A Coast Guard launch had pulled into Swartz Bay where the planes were moored in the shelter of Piers Island.

The Canadian officer had been curious, but nevertheless remarkably polite in enquiring into the reason for their presence. He had died with his crew of two for his curiosity; Turinsk felt no regret — American officials were plentiful, a nuisance and expendable.

After the raid on the *Fraser* had been carried out and success seemed certain, one of the planes had developed engine trouble forcing the escape party to land at the Queen Charlottes to effect repairs.

Now only the sick plane remained and two of their party were dead, one drowned after being hit by an oil drum, the other shot through the head. The unfortunate man who had been hit by rifle fire from the shore had been one of the two who were able to pilot the amphibians.

Seven of them remained stranded with a single aircraft and one pilot.

It had been ironical that the bombing had smashed the fuselage of the good float plane — Turinsk had been close to despair when the tragedy occurred.

Two engineers from the *Vertaz* were now desperately trying to discover the fault in the fuel system which prevented the aircraft from developing more than about two-thirds of its rated power.

If they had limped on whilst airborne, Turinsk thought ruefully, they could be 2,500 miles north by now — he must have been an idiot to have listened to that stupid old fool of a professor.

Help must soon follow for the helicopter: on the island, the men armed with rifles would certainly have some form of boat enabling them to cross to the mainland, and then there was the helicopter crew. If Turinsk could not escape before sunrise there would be no hope.

'Hurry, hurry,' he snapped at the men for the hundredth time.

Just before it became dark, Chkalov and Professor Petrov had waded to the shore. They had been arguing there ever since. Turinsk could hear their voices across the water now and then.

He spoke loudly enough for his words to carry to the beach, 'Comrades, it would be wise to be as quiet as possible.'

There was no answer from the two men, but afterwards Turinsk could no longer hear their voices.

A clang echoed from the front of the plane followed by some angry conversation, signs of strain were beginning to show.

None of them had any illusions about their fate should the amphibian fail to be repaired. As well as exposed Soviet agents, the trail of killings since they had left California branded them as particularly violent criminals and the Americans were not likely to be lenient.

Assailed with cowardly thoughts, Turinsk selfishly began to consider means of saving his own skin. He knew he would now never be safe anywhere in North America and he could hardly return to Russia after such a dismal performance — retribution would be swift and cruel. Suicide or the remote chance of obtaining political asylum in a neutral country remained his only hope.

On the shore Professor Petrov had also reached the end of his particular emotional tether.

'I am a scientist — not an adventurer or a murderer,' he whispered to Chkalov. 'I am not accustomed to this sort of thing.'

Chkalov laughed shortly.

'Well you're part of it aren't you?' he had started to despise the older man.

The professor shivered.

He said, 'I am sure we shall be caught. It would have been better to have carried on to Vancouver.'

Chkalov said, 'You're as bad as Turinsk, you think the Americans are fools. If you had worked in the States as long as I have you would not wish you had landed.'

Someone came paddling from the

aircraft. It was Turinsk.

'The feed pipe is partially blocked,' he said, 'We are going to replace the whole section with some piping from the extinguishing system if Raslitz cannot free the obstruction, but we will have to wait for the moon before we can start work.'

Petrov glanced up from where he was sitting.

'And if it clouds over?' he asked.

Turinsk answered him angrily, 'Then, Professor Petrov, we will have to make do in the dark, or with the ineffective short lead light we have made.'

Chkalov said, 'Be careful you don't run down the batteries with the light.'

Turinsk was conscious that Chkalov was a highly experienced, competent and well-thought-of agent; he had been treating him accordingly since the failure of the plane had occurred.

'Comrade Chkalov,' he said, 'The men from the island are certainly on their way here, and perhaps some of the crew from the helicopter will attempt to stop us. I would take it as a favour if you would advise us of the best defence tactics and positions.'

Chkalov said, 'You believe we will have to fight our way off?'

Turinsk was surprised. He said, 'Yes I do.'

Chkalov said, 'So do I, Comrade, come, let us plan.'

They began to speak earnestly together in the dark ignoring the silent professor sitting miserably on a flat rock his head resting on his cupped hands.

Later in the evening, preparations were interrupted by the distant buzzing of a small outboard, traversing the coast some way out on the still water between the island and their camp.

Turinsk strained his eyes until they smarted. He could see nothing.

Chkalov said, 'It will be the men from the island — they know very well where we are; they will land up coast and come to meet us on foot. I think they will be surprised comrade.' He lifted a submachine gun in each hand.

'Also I think we will make our escape after all, but we must hope these

Canadians do not call their silly Air Force. We have sharp teeth for fighting on land, but nothing for the air.'

★ ★ ★

Slowly the semi-circular yellow moon rose in a cloudless sky illuminating an unusually busy section of British Columbian coastline.

Trevor Sand said, 'Over there, by that dark bulge.'

He pointed with his right hand to a sinister dark outcrop of rock rising from the relative lowness of the area they were passing in the boat.

Otis Corder swivelled the Seagull on the transome, feeling the heavy boat respond sluggishly. He throttled the outboard back to half speed, they didn't want wet feet from a splintered hole in the bottom. In the dim moonlight, dark rocks protruded from the water all around them.

Sand had timed his move well. The group had left the island late enough to putter past the stranded Russians whilst it was still dark, but now, probably less than half a mile away from the plane, there was sufficient light to choose somewhere to land.

The noise of the outboard engine would obviously have been heard by the encamped Soviets, but Sand wanted to make sure he wasn't seen in case he had badly misjudged the distance from the shore inadvertently coming within range of the Russians' guns.

Since the brief exchange of shots whilst the helicopter was unloading oil drums, Sand had been attempting to decide on his next move. His men had urged him to follow the crippled amphibian as it taxied away from the island carrying all the communists. When it stopped again at the mainland, Sand guessed that he had at least the night to work in.

Firstly, they had crossed the narrow Straits to where the helicopter had landed, hoping that the reason for the sudden dive was purely mechanical rather than an indication of any injury to either Donahue or the pilot Phil.

One of the Canadians — Graham

Nelson, who had received some formal medical training in the army, checked over the still unconscious pilot, subsequently putting through a duplicate call to Control on the Iroquois radio. He proved luckier than Donahue, a reply was received at once. It was a very rude reply saying that a doctor was already on his way following the first request for assistance. Of more importance was the news that seventy-five airborne troops would leave at daylight to be parachuted into the area. Sand was told that it was his responsibility to hold the communists until morning — nothing else.

He was unable to tell Control where Donahue was.

Later, just before midnight, they had left the helicopter, cruising north past the Russians in order to close in on them from two sides, Sands judging accurately that Donahue would already be moving towards Chkalov from the south.

Corder pivoted the outboard upwards as the bows of the boat crunched gently on a pebble bank. They were going to have to wade after all.

One by one the men removed boots and socks before climbing over the side into the black water, each making a series of miniature ripples that broke without sound on the shore in front of them.

Once the party was assembled, Sand briefed his men. In a few minutes, in single file, they started to walk slowly between the clumps of dry seaweed and piles of white driftwood.

Under the cloak of darkness an Englishman and four Canadians converged on seven desperate Russians who were expecting them.

16

Just enough moonlight filtered through the branches of the trees for him to see his watch providing he held it sufficiently close to his face. The ticking sounded remarkably loud.

Now and again a small wave would lap on the shore but, for the most part, the greatest noise was that caused by his own passage along the beach.

This was the third or fourth beach he had encountered. In between there had been mostly a mixture of eroding slippery soil sometimes covered in matted reeds and scrub. At two points, Donahue had crawled on ledges along the base of low cliffs or jumped from boulder to boulder, slipping so many times he had lost count. It was incredible that such a variety of terrain could be packed into such a short strip of coast.

From here on he knew that he must observe extreme caution and, above all, be quiet when he moved. There had not been much time to memorize the part of the coast he could see from the helicopter. Also, he had always found it hard to judge how far he'd travelled in cover like this. Nevertheless, the little line of rocks gleaming away from a low promontory ahead of him seemed to be a recognizable landmark.

Donahue thought that he had been lucky to find the tide on its way out.

Chkalov's camp would lie in the next sweeping curve of the shore if his memory had not failed him. It was necessary to be sure.

Donahue took off his shoes, walking very softly, avoiding any dark or light patches that he could see on the sand. Before putting weight on either foot, he tested the ground carefully: one snap from a driftwood branch would alert any trained ear, even though the listener could be perhaps as far as a quarter of a mile away.

Stepping gingerly onto the first and largest rock of the chain, he flattened against the damp crumbling cliff face.

An earthy smell filled his nostrils.

Two hundred and fifty yards away shone the pale whiteness of the amphibian, a dim glow radiating from the far side of the engine nacelle. Two men were working with their backs to him. Donahue could hear them speaking.

He watched for a long time, straining his tired eyes for any sign of the others who he supposed would be close at hand on the shore somewhere.

Donahue thought that anybody coming upon the Russians by way of the beach would be dead before he knew it.

He watched for a moment longer before retiring to the beach where he wrung out his socks and replaced the shoes which were showing signs of extreme strain by now.

Enough time remained to find a better way before daylight. He was hungry and both his neck and leg were aching slightly, the latter in an unpleasant if familiar way; if he stopped now, it would stiffen up at once.

Donahue backtracked until he found what appeared to be an opening into the forest. No game trails led to the beach and there were no stream beds, although he passed several of these on other beaches he had crossed.

Following the rudiments of an old natural track of some kind, he began to climb. Underfoot, the ground was soft making it relatively easy to move quietly although, under the trees, the light was extremely poor.

The slope was severe, quickly flattening out onto a low ridge forming the forests main defence against the sea. Some prairie grass grew in patches in the small clearing where he stood.

It was difficult for him to make absolutely sure that he was not silhouetted against the horizon behind, it was even possible that his figure would contrast with the blackness of the big trees surrounding three sides of the miniature prairie.

If Chkalov was as experienced as Donahue believed, half a mistake would be enough to gain a swift death. He could not afford the smallest error.

This time, Simon Donahue was not

afraid; he was too busy, too involved and totally absorbed in what he was doing. He felt clear-headed and alert. In short, he had become adapted to stress.

He would have to move from the clearing before making his way as best he could through the mass of trees towards the Russians' base. Luckily the ground was flat, even perhaps a little downhill for the two hundred yards or so that he would have to travel.

To walk in open country with a strung hunting bow is a simple matter despite the fact that it may be five feet in length and slightly curved. In dense brush it quickly becomes impossible. Small branches snag in the narrowing gaps formed between bow string and nock whilst the shape seems to be especially designed for maximum inconvenience. There are numerous aids for the bowhunter, designed to obviate this problem — none are satisfactory.

Long experience had taught Donahue that it is necessary to completely remove the string from the bow, leaving only a smooth polished stave to manoeuvre through the woods.

Apart from the knife he had taken from the helicopter pilot an unstrung bow left him defenceless.

Arrows were somewhat less of a problem. A wrapped handkerchief protected the honed razor heads, the slim bundle being thrust down the back of his shirt. The flights were arrayed behind his head, and providing he exercised reasonable care, they would not be damaged unless he was forced to duck suddenly in order to avoid a branch or some other obstacle.

Once inside the brush, which fortunately proved to be less dense than it had appeared from the ridge, Donahue proceeded with utmost caution, feeding the bow through the tangle of vegetation before him.

Then, after a particularly bad patch of twenty or thirty yards of an almost impenetrable barrier of saplings, he chanced upon what seemed to be a trail. Whilst he could not be certain, it could possibly be the same track that he had followed up the incline from the beach. Conceivably, it would have been made long ago by rabbits or even deer, although the larger animals could not have used it for some time. In the almost totally obscured light from the half moon, there was no way of identifying past users of the track; it was very nearly impossible to detect its presence at all as it meandered around the exposed roots of trees and through the grass and leaves matting the damp ground.

The first fifty yards took him forty minutes to negotiate.

It had become essential to follow the vague trail; if he lost it, a solid wall of branches and young trees loomed up in the blackness at once. He began to wonder if it would have been worth risking the straightforward route along the beach.

Panting slightly, he paused for thought; what would Chkalov expect him to do?

Earlier, Donahue had heard the outboard pass by out on the water, guessing that it was Trevor Sand and the others. Like Chkalov, he thought the Canadians would land a short distance north of the Russians hoping that Donahue would be approaching from the south. Of course, Sand could have no real idea of Donahue's intentions. Similarly, Donahue had no way of knowing what Trevor Sand had decided to do. It was a dangerous game that they were playing.

Chkalov would not be stupid enough to post guards only on the obvious access points to their camp, the trick therefore would be to out-guess each other.

Inside the next one hundred and fifty yards Donahue expected to come upon some evidence to indicate the presence of a watcher. Somehow or other the position of this sentry must be pin-pointed before he heard or saw Donahue.

His luck improved. The trail became more definite and the trees loftier allowing a little more moonlight to filter through. It was easier to see but also easier to be seen.

Donahue wondered if Chkalov had found the path too. If he had, it was possible he could blunder right into the lap of a waiting Russian.

Under these circumstances there was only one thing to do. It required infinite patience coupled with concentration of such rigidity that he knew it could be sustained only for an hour or two at the very most.

Twenty minutes later — as far as he could judge under such awkward conditions — he had travelled a further fifty yards. In a few minutes his vigil must begin.

Since his association with Seven Nine, only twice before had he embarked on this form of intense wait; once in East Germany in the snow, half way up a mountain one January, and once in Spain in the middle of a corn field on a summer night like this.

The principle was simple. Anxious to detect the presence of the sentry, he had to move to a fixed position where he must remain absolutely silent and motionless, facing in the direction of the suspected enemy. The winner of the game is he who detects the other first. Perhaps childish in conception, the results are invariably deadly. It is common for the loser to pay with his life.

Donahue's problem was magnified a hundredfold, not only because he had to establish his position by moving to it first, but because his weapon could not easily be made ready beforehand. He realized it would be of no use discovering the location of the Russian if he was unable to silence the man. To move through this stuff until close enough to use the knife would be a physical impossibility. He must be able to kill from a distance.

He strung the powerful bow making quite sure that the string was secure in each nock by carefully exploring the outline with his fingertips.

Leaving his right hand free to clear a path through the trees, against the bow, two each side he clasped the slender arrows.

Now came the dangerous part. He had to move forwards to a selected position where he could settle, wait, watch and listen. Under dry conditions it would have been suicide to attempt such a journey. With extreme stealth and causing only two slight rustlings when his clothing snagged on twigs, in about half an hour he was ready.

It was possible that the place he had chosen would be too exposed under lighter conditions; however, in the yellow paleness of the moonlight it seemed admirable.

Through the trees to his left floated the aircraft whilst in front the forest thinned to yet another clearing.

Chkalov would have chosen this place because of the clearing. Without being seen it would be difficult if not impossible for anyone to approach closer than twenty feet from the centre of the almost circular patch of scrub.

Feeling as though fine sand had been thrown in them, Donahue's eyes had been straining now for over half the night. They were in no fit state to begin a further stretch of watching. He blinked several times to clear the tears.

It was disturbing that he was unable to see any sign of the eight communists that he was sure must be somewhere on the beach or in the clearing.

Fifteen minutes later, far away to the

south, he heard the characteristic beating of a helicopter.

Several seconds elapsed before he realized that it would be help for the wounded pilot; Vancouver would have sent a doctor maybe half an hour after Donahue had radioed. The time was exactly correct.

The fact that Donahue had been able to identify the sound at once, as well as knowing why a helicopter should be flying up the coast at this time of night, gave him a brief advantage.

In the far right of his peripheral vision, something moved.

Very slowly, he turned his head riveting his attention on the dark shadow of a rotten tree stump on the edge of the clearing.

Again the shadow distorted sideways. Donahue had found the sentry.

Now he could see the outline of the man, sitting back against the stump, an automatic rifle resting across his knees. Donahue flicked his eyes to the beach, then scanned back to the sentry; if the man had not been so foolish a moment ago he would have remained lost in the shadows and dark patches of the background.

The noise from the helicopter grew louder. By now the crew should easily be able to see the lights of the Iroquois on the beach; Donahue thought that landing near to it in the dark without ending up in the water would be difficult. He knew the beach was not large enough for two of the unwieldy aircraft.

The Russian sentry was obviously alarmed; he stood up.

Donahue made a rapid decision — changed his mind twice — then acted.

The fine edges of the steel razor head sliced easily through the neck, cut the jugular vein and half severed the vertebrae. Finally the feathers arrested the deadly path of the smooth arrow. It had taken the man squarely in the throat.

There was a faint cough followed by a bubbling noise. The man toppled silently onto a soft bed of damp leaves. Donahue was not watching the man.

The white flicker of the feathers under the dim outline of the Russian's head told Donahue that there would be no sound other than the thud as he hit the ground. If he fell noisily it would alert the others. There was no other movement in the clearing following the gentle collapse of the dead communist. The silence was oppressive.

Elevation is difficult to master with a long bow, Donahue knew that it had been a lucky shot — if he had aimed a fraction lower the man could easily have screamed as the arrow entered his body. Or the sentry could have fallen into the brittle tangle of dead branches to his left causing enough noise to bring all the Russians to the scene. Instead, everything had been perfect.

Now he must find the other sentries that Chkalov would have posted. Somewhere hidden, in the dark out there, men were waiting for Donahue.

One of them — perhaps an engineer from the *Vertaz* — unaccustomed to this work and not conscious of the seriousness of his job made a classic mistake. The shielding of the flame from the lighter was nearly perfect and afterwards Donahue only once saw the dull glow from the burning cigarette tip. It was the click that had attracted the attention of the archer but there was no other visible sign of the careful smoker.

At sixty yards the range was too great in moonlight besides being impossible without a silhouette to aim at.

Donahue watched.

After his eyes became so filled with tears that there was no practical purpose in continuing he directed his attention to the seaplane, the change in range coming as a slight but no less welcome relief.

Simon Donahue knew that he could not carry on much longer. Before eyes and his stiffening body failed, he would have to force their hand. From here on his life would depend on his skill.

This time, although at a greater distance, the shot was easier.

The white painted aluminium alloy of the plane formed a perfect background. Across Donahue's shoulders the sinews contracted as the hook formed by his fingers took the strain of the bow string.

It was pure murder.

The arrowhead penetrated the aircraft skin, pinning the man to the fuselage. Unable to move, his agonized twisting slowly diminished until he hung limply, impaled on the arrow passing through his trunk.

Working alongside, standing on the pontoon of the undercarriage, his colleague panicked, jumping backwards into the shallow water where, shouting loudly, he started to run towards the beach.

Donahue's third arrow struck him horribly in the stomach. He screamed like a wounded animal continuing his headlong run until he fell squirming onto the sand trying ineffectively to pull the sharpened barb from his entrails.

For a moment Donahue was sickened by the sight; it had been a snap shot, hurried too much and poorly aimed.

His compassion evaporated as two machine guns burst angrily into life across the clearing. Men were shouting between bursts and everywhere there was crashing in the undergrowth. Acrid smoke from burnt cordite hung in the air wreathing like ghosts in the moonlight.

Bullets ricocheted from the tree that Donahue had kept to his rear. He must evacuate his present position at once.

Each time the guns flashed, filling the forest with their fearful noise, Donahue moved sharply forward through dense brush to where the first sentry lay.

When he was nearly there the man with the cigarette stood up — a perfect close range target. With his last arrow Donahue shot him calmly and mercilessly in the face.

Unscathed, Donahue reached the first sentry. Before picking up the submachine gun lying beside the body he pulled the arrow on through the neck, wiping blood from the flights on his handkerchief to dry them.

Firing randomly at shadows, the Russians had obviously realized that the bowman was hidden on the southern border of the clearing. Bullets whined into the soil behind Donahue.

With his long cruel arrows he had killed four men. One arrow had been retrieved and now he had a firearm. He inspected the weapon, an American Armalite AR15 capable of fully automatic operation and fitted with a folding stock for compactness. A useful gun now that the silence of the bow was of advantage no longer.

Suddenly, his movements caused a series of bursts of fire to flare from the beach. Bullets spattered bark and wood chips into his face, violently smashing into trees each side of him. Now two guns were shooting from the waters edge — Donahue guessed that all of the Russians must have been recalled from the clearing.

Bow in one hand, submachine gun in the other, he wormed his way on his belly back into the protection of the woods.

It was nearly dawn.

At high water line, Turinsk shouted angrily at the small man.

'You know this Englishman with the arrows — you knew he would come — why in God's name did you put Raslitz on the south side? On the other side he would have seen him coming!'

Chkalov ignored the outburst.

He said, 'Get your pilot and the professor into the plane — they'll be safe from arrows there. Then tie up the loose ends on the fuel pipe while I cover you.'

Wearily, making himself comfortable behind a substantial log, Chkalov flicked off the safety of the Armalite waiting pointedly for Turinsk to move away.

'Go on,' he snarled, 'or the sun will be too high for us.'

Chkalov was afraid. Although it had now been many years since he had been forced to use physical violence, in street fighting, in dark alleys or in buildings, the Russian had been masterful. In these quiet forest glades, against a man with a weapon that was obsolete four hundred years ago, Chkalov was helpless.

He waited, watching the trees.

Then Turinsk was shouting at him from the plane. He had pulled the dead mechanic from the arrow leaving the body floating alongside the plane.

'It's done comrade!'

Chkalov could see the aircraft clearly

now, dawn was breaking quickly, in ten minutes there would be plenty of light — perhaps too much.

He glanced back at the trees. If he moved now, an arrow could fly at him from anywhere.

Suddenly four men ran from the north edge of the clearing.

Squeezing the trigger, he moved the gun, feeling it buck hard against his shoulder as the deadly hail of lead sprayed up the foreshore towards the trees. Little spurts of earth followed one man, failing to overtake the figure before it reached the protection of a tall pine.

Behind him the amphibian's starter began to whine, in seconds the engine sputtering into life. Grains of sand, whipped up by the draught from the propellor stung the back of his head.

Chkalov turned knowing he had been deserted.

The aircraft accelerated across the flat calmness of the water. Turinsk was not inside, he hung desperately to the fuselage trying to open the door.

Panicking at the gunfire, Petrov had

ordered the pilot to take off immediately Turinsk had finished the repair.

Hidden in the trees, Trevor Sand ordered his men to fire at the retreating plane leaving Donahue to exhaust the magazine on his Armalite by firing into the log behind which Chkalov was crouched.

Soon the amphibian became airborne, sweeping immediately to the right over an extensive area of rocks exposed by the low tide. With its light load it quickly gained altitude.

A tiny speck became detached from the side of the plane. It fell with a twisting motion end over end onto the jagged stones at the foot of a bleak grey cliff.

Simultaneously, at tree top height, an Iroquois howled across the grass prairie, its ugly green body tilted downwards at the nose, as it pursued the fleeing Russians.

The pilot straightened the helicopter, climbed and closed the gap on the sluggish float plane ahead of him.

Red flames spurted from the underside of the Iroquois as two Red Top rockets were unleashed from their launch tubes.

A brilliant ball of orange fire glowed briefly in the grey of the July morning. As it died, pieces of burning aircraft cascaded into the sea leaving whisps of smoke drifting gently towards the north, gradually diffusing to nothing or mixing with the mist rising from the water.

When it was all over, Donahue shouted.

'Come on Chkalov — out.'

The solitary Russian rose from the cover of the log, Armalite held loosely in his right hand, muzzle pointing to the ground.

'Leave it there,' Sand ordered.

Chkalov dropped the gun and stood waiting, hands at his side — a pathetic small figure alone on the beach.

Donahue said, 'Away from it, Chkalov,' and began walking down the grassy incline to the water.

When he reached the Russian he stared into sullen eyes filled with fear and hate.

Donahue said softly, 'It's tough comrade, very tough.'

Overhead, a Canadian Air Force Argosy of Coastal Command circled slowly, her pilot listening to the message being transmitted by the Iroquois which had returned to hover high over the group of men below.

As if disappointed the troop carrier broke her course, droning away steadily towards home, carrying the men that had not been needed.

17

'I don't know what you're complaining about,' Colin Miller spoke enviously, 'I have to do it all the time.'

Donahue didn't have his own office at Seven Nine headquarters in Threadneedle Street anymore. An Army Captain had taken it over temporarily for some obscure purpose that no-one would tell him about. Not that it mattered. Donahue found offices dreary places to be avoided whenever possible.

He sat at a borrowed desk in Miller's office on the second floor, sucking a pencil and looking utterly bored. Four pages of handwritten notes were scattered untidily over the blotter.

Donahue said, 'I've told the story so many times to so many people, I sound like a cheap paperback. They've got it on tape, there are photographs of everybody and everything remotely connected with the whole thing, and now I've got to write it down. I shall never understand why something classified as Secret has to be recorded so many ways and in so many places that it can't possibly be kept secret.'

'Do you want me to write it for you?' Miller asked, 'All you have to do is to tell me about what happened and I'll whip it into shape.'

Donahue shook his head. 'You know I'm not supposed to tell anyone except Goddard.'

Miller laughed. 'But I'll get a copy of your report — if you ever finish it.'

Pushing his chair back, Donahue lit his tenth cigarette of the day tossing the packet over to his friend.

'Of course I'll finish it,' he said. 'I've finished all the others haven't I?'

Miller was still grinning. 'You better get on with it then, don't you think.'

He returned the packet of cigarettes Donahue had bought on the plane and left the room.

Donahue clasped both hands behind his head, closed his eyes and tried to think of how to tie up the loose ends.

British Columbia seemed a long way away and the violence on the quiet deserted beaches that had taken place only days ago were unreal and unpleasant memories. He didn't want to think about them, let alone write an analytical account of the events for the files of Seven Nine.

★ ★ ★

When the hovering Iroquois landed in the clearing, Chkalov had been escorted to it where he was handcuffed to a seat in the rear.

The pilot informed Donahue that Mansfield wanted him to accompany the Russian back to Vancouver. Request or order, Donahue didn't care which. It was certainly the quickest way back to civilization which was all he cared about.

His need for food and rest had become critical now that everything was over. He was washed out and thoroughly sickened by what he had done and what he had seen.

In the morning light the men he had killed were scattered grotesquely all round the miniature clearing. The Russian that had been impaled against the amphibian, to be later pulled away by Turinsk, floated at the waters edge, a red stain spreading thinly from his body to the sand. A short distance away, the man who had been shot through the stomach, lay in a hunched position on his side. It had taken him a long time to die.

Leaving Trevor Sand and his men to clear up the mess, Donahue climbed gratefully into the helicopter fastening himself into the seat next to Chkalov who appeared even more fatigued than Donahue himself.

Both men slept whilst the Iroquois flew down the coast. On a stretcher behind the cockpit the pilot of the first helicopter watched the Russian and the Englishman sleeping. His wound was serious but it was by no means a permanent injury. Phil thought he had been pretty lucky.

In the navigator's seat the army doctor that had been sent by Mansfield wondered what on earth had been going on along the two mile stretch of beach he had just visited.

There was no conversation.

They landed at a military airfield near Westwood where Chkalov was taken by armed guard to the Army Section of Canadian Intelligence. Donahue never saw him again.

Goddard had not known whether to congratulate Donahue or not. Although Chkalov had been captured, all the other communists were dead — perhaps things could have been handled better? Goddard would never know.

Again, there had been endless questions in Mansfield's office. Then the flight home via Montreal where Donahue stopped over for two days to break the journey. Francis Goddard returned directly to London.

Donahue had telephoned Jane from Heathrow to say he was back. He wouldn't be able to see her until the weekend — his job was not quite finished.

★ ★ ★

It was Friday. His report should have been finished yesterday, Goddard had to take it to MI4 this afternoon — typed.

Donahue started to scribble furiously.

After an hour and a half he reached for the telephone on Miller's desk.

He said, 'It's ready Mrs Lorraine. I shall be in Farnham if anyone wants me but don't spread it around.'

He grinned at the answer from the Senior Secretary of Seven Nine, replaced the receiver, tidied his desk and walked quickly from the office, leaving the door open.

Donahue didn't go to Farnham. Goddard might have more questions and Donahue certainly was not returning to London.

Jane had wanted him to take a holiday in the West Country — at Ilfracombe. No matter how quaint or picturesque, Donahue had seen enough beaches to last him a very long time. Similarly, the idea of spending time anywhere by the sea was not attractive. No, and he didn't want to fly to the Mediterranean either, the thought of another journey by air was abhorrent to him.

Jane Marshall wondered where he could have been since the middle of July to make him so reluctant to comply with her suggestions. Usually they would have been met with enthusiasm.

In the three telephone conversations with Simon since he had arrived home she had avoided asking about his trip. Finally, after he had rejected all her ideas, she had told him in exasperation that anywhere he decided they should go would be fine with her and left it at that.

On Thursday evening Simon had telephoned as arranged at eight o'clock. His instructions were a little mysterious. On Friday, Jane was to drive to Aldershot railway station in the Alfa Romeo with everything packed for a two week holiday. She would leave the car there and catch the 5.05 direct to Waterloo where Donahue would be waiting for her.

At ten minutes past six she stepped down from the train and mingled with the crowd shuffling towards the ticket collector.

Donahue was leaning idly against the barrier.

Jane's heart leapt. There were too many people in the way — she pushed through a gap between two gentlemen carrying brief cases and rolled umbrellas.

'Simon,' she cried.

His lean face turned towards her, smiling as the slight girl rushed headlong into his arms.

'Oh Simon.'

Scenes of this kind are not unusual on railway stations. The ticket collector ignored the couple as did the majority of the passengers passing through the exit gate.

Donahue held her tightly, his head buried in her hair. Jane was crying.

He said gruffly. 'You were crying the last time I saw you.'

'I've been worried about you.'

'There was no need.'

'That man I saw when I was up here last — Mr Goddard — '

Donahue interrupted, 'Forget all about

that, and we are not going to talk about any Mr Goddard. Come on.'

He pulled her arms away, propelling her through the barrier. The ticket collector said, 'Good-night Miss,' not bothering to take the stub.

When they were clear of the crowd, Jane stopped.

'Simon, don't make fun of me.'

'I'm not.'

He was dressed in a lightweight sports jacket worn over a pale blue polo-necked sweater. The lines in his face were deeper than she remembered and he looked tired.

She said, 'I want to know where you've been.'

'Goddard told you — Vancouver.'

'What for?'

Donahue put his hands on her shoulders and looked into her big eyes, tears still trapped in the corners.

'Jane, I can't tell you and if I could I wouldn't. You know all about that — I know you do. Please don't ask me. I'm back, we're together, we have two weeks and I love you very much.'

She stared back at him for a while.

'Will you be going away again?'

'No.'

'Do you promise?'

'I promise.'

'Liar,' she laughed suddenly, 'all right.'

She pulled Donahue to the taxi rank. 'Where are you taking me?'

They ate at a small Indian restaurant that Simon had taken her to once before. At half past eight they took another taxi to Piccadilly.

'I know it's not really a glamorous night out,' he said, 'but I rather want to see it and you might like it too.'

They saw a re-run of Arthur Clarke's movie '2001 A Space Odyssey'. Jane thought it was wonderful but didn't understand much of the story. Donahue was quiet when they left the cinema and walked out into the lights.

'What made you want to see it Simon?'

'Because it's unreal, because it couldn't happen yet.'

'That doesn't explain.'

'It couldn't happen to me.'

'Of course it couldn't — but so what?'

Donahue flagged down a taxi and said, 'Waterloo,' through the window to the driver.

As they drove through the swirling lights of London's night traffic, he spoke quietly to Jane.

'Janey, I've had a bit of a tough time. I wanted to see a film that was about something very, very different — that's all.'

'Oh.'

He put his arm round her.

At the station they boarded the late train back to Aldershot. Jane slept for most of the way. It was half past one by the time Donahue swung the small blue sports car out of the car park, its Abarth exhaust echoing along the deserted streets of the Army town.

The girl snuggled down into the bucket seat, one hand resting loosely on the grab rail watching the powerful beams of the headlights sweep the road ahead.

Soon the Alfa was travelling on the new Winchester bypass, Donahue cutting each curve as he increased the speed of the swiftly moving car.

Before they knew it, Southampton had disappeared behind them into the night.

On the east borders of the New Forest he wound up the little overhead cam engine until finally, at six thousand on the rev counter, the Alfa sped through the dark at the magic ton.

He enjoyed driving at night and in a superb machine like the Italian Alfa he became one with the vehicle, utterly committed to the task in hand.

Jane was surprised — even a little disappointed when they slowed at the edge of the pretty village of Lyndhurst, turning right half way along the main street on the road to Stoney Cross.

Less than a mile from the intersection, Donahue pulled into the gravel driveway of a small hotel.

'We're here, kid.'

'Where?'

'Where we're going to have our holiday.'

'I can't see it in the dark — is it nice?'

'Very nice.'

It was an extremely small hotel.

Donahue had to carry Jane's luggage upstairs. In their room, which was very pleasant if rather small, Donahue's three cases already lay on the double bed.

'I had them sent on,' he explained.

Jane said, 'Could we have some sandwiches Simon — please?'

'At this time of night!'

'Please darling, I'm hungry.'

He closed the bedroom door quietly behind him hoping that the staff were not all in bed yet.

Half an hour later, a bottle of Mateus Rosé and two glasses in one hand and a plate of ham sandwiches precariously balanced in the other, he was back.

He whispered, 'Jane, it's me — open the door.'

'It's not on the catch, push.'

Donahue pushed.

Jane Marshall lay on the bed, the covers turned back. At first Donahue thought she was naked, then he saw the thin nightdress of some filmy transparent material covering her full young body.

She said, 'Hadn't you better close the door?'

He put the wine and sandwiches unsteadily on the table, feeling his body start to react uncontrollably.

'Can we have the wine afterwards Simon?' her voice was husky.

The bottle was still unopened in the morning and the sandwiches were stale.

When she woke up, Donahue had gone. Outside it was a wonderful day. Sunshine poured through the bedroom windows and the air was warm already. She felt very happy.

He returned as she finished dressing.

'Hi,' he said.

'Good morning Mr Donahue. I thought you had loved me and left me.'

'I had to go to Lyndhurst.'

'Oh.'

He swung her round by the waist, almost lifting her feet from the carpet.

He said, 'Breakfast.'

When they had eaten they returned upstairs to unpack their things properly. He removed a long leather tube from the wardrobe.

'You know that film we saw?' he asked.

'I haven't forgotten already.'

'I said I wanted to see it because of making me forget — you know.'

'Yes.'

'There's one more thing I've got to do.'

'With your bow?'

'I'm afraid so.'

'Simon — I wish I understood.'

'I've bought you a present.'

'Oh, and I haven't got you anything.' She looked upset.

'It's not very exciting,' he withdrew a cardboard box from beneath the bed. It was a very long box.

Jane lifted the lid. She didn't know what to say.

Donahue smiled at her, 'It's so as you can help me.'

She took out a bow.

He said, 'It's laminated maple.'

'Is that good?'

'It's only twenty-five pounds, you'll be able to pull it easily.'

Three hours later on the summer morning they were walking down a road of yellow gravel through a fenced area of the New Forest, normally out of bounds to campers or hikers. Donahue had obtained special permission to enter the reserve. The man at Lyndhurst had understood perfectly.

Roving is a pastime rarely practised today. It is an idle pursuit which accomplishes nothing but affords a great deal of pleasure to the archers who play it. The leader shoots an arrow at any target he pleases. Others of the party endeavour to shoot their arrows at precisely the same point. He who comes the closest gains the honour of choosing the next target. No one can win and no one can lose. It is very relaxing and quite pointless.

Donahue was sweating as he pulled back the bow string for the first shot. His hand trembled uncontrollably. Before him were men, not trees. He loosed the arrow watching the searing flight take it to the base of a large oak.

Awkwardly, Jane let her arrow fly. It quivered in another tree, ten feet above the ground.

She said, 'Oh dear,' putting a hand to her mouth.

The only way to retrieve it was for her to sit on Donahue's shoulders whilst he lifted her up.

They were both laughing by the time they were ready to move on. He let her shoot first.

Jane improved quickly. To her surprise she enjoyed it although the string hurt the tips of her fingers after a while.

Before all the cheap cedar arrows had been either lost or broken Donahue had rid himself of his memories. Archery meant too much to him to have it spoilt forever by recollections of the past. Now, after this morning with Jane the fears had gone — perhaps not forever but for long enough to fade in vividness. In time he would forget completely.

For the next two weeks in the sunshine and inevitably in the rain as well, they did nothing that was not for themselves. It was a time of great happiness for both people.

We do hope that you have enjoyed reading this large print book.

Did you know that all of our titles are available for purchase?

We publish a wide range of high quality large print books including:

Romances, Mysteries, Classics
General Fiction
Non Fiction and Westerns

Special interest titles available in large print are:

The Little Oxford Dictionary
Music Book, Song Book
Hymn Book, Service Book

Also available from us courtesy of Oxford University Press:

Young Readers' Dictionary
(large print edition)
Young Readers' Thesaurus
(large print edition)

For further information or a free brochure, please contact us at:
Ulverscroft Large Print Books Ltd.,
The Green, Bradgate Road, Anstey,
Leicester, LE7 7FU, England.
Tel: (00 44) **0116 236 4325**
Fax: (00 44) **0116 234 0205**

DEAD BEFORE MIDNIGHT

Robert Charles

When Sandra Bishop is found strangled in the boot of a burned-out car, suspicion automatically falls upon Dennis Hamilton, the man at the wheel when the crash occurred. Hamilton, the author of a dozen crime novels, is suddenly caught up in a tangled mesh of events of the kind he normally creates. Then, he goes on the run and his behaviour becomes irrational. Another girl is murdered, and a vast manhunt is launched through the Breckland forests . . .

LAKESIDE ZERO

Douglas Enefer

It looks like a clear case of murder by stabbing, perpetrated by a teenage gang gate-crashing a private party. But Liverpool police detective Sam Bawtry, who is always apt to see beyond the obvious when investigating crime, isn't convinced. He sets out, with little official backing, to uncover more than circumstantial evidence — and finds himself in a maze of seemingly disconnected intrigue. In the end, he faces a macabre challenge.

SIDEWINDER

Jane Morell

Lisette, a British agent sent to the Lebanon to extricate an American hostage, disappears without trace, leaving behind a husband and a young son, Robert. Ten years later, Robert tracks down her betrayer, intent on revenge. Winton, the man responsible, has made a new life for himself in Wales. However, Robert doesn't count on meeting Winton's daughter, Sara. How can he murder the father of the girl he has come to love? But is Sara the innocent creature she appears to be?